shooting**fish**

Dylan was on a high and wasn't in the mood for discussing the piffling amounts of money he had promised Georgie. Not when they had just made the decidedly unpiffling amount of one hundred thousand pounds. 'Can you believe it back there?' he said to Jez. 'It was like shooting fish.'

'Shooting fish?'

'Yeah. In a barrel.'

Jez frowned. The language barrier, even after five years, hadn't quite been demolished. 'What's that mean?'

'Uh ... well...' This time Dylan frowned. The words *swindle, defraud, rip-off with ease* seemed so crass. Especially in front of a nice girl like Georgie.

'It means,' piped up Georgie from behind them, 'that it's really easy to rip people off. To swindle and defraud them. Easy and fun.'

'Wasn't that easy,' objected a miffed Dylan. 'We put a lot of work into that operation.'

*shooting***fish**

a novel by Graeme Grant

from the screenplay by Stefan Schwartz
and Richard Holmes

HarperCollins*Publishers*

HarperCollins*Publishers*
77–85 Fulham Palace Road,
Hammersmith, London W6 8JB

A Paperback Original 1997
1 3 5 7 9 8 6 4 2

Copyright © Stefan Schwartz and Richard Holmes 1997

A catalogue record for this book is
available from the British Library

ISBN 0 00 651116 3

Set in Fairfield Light by
Rowland Phototypesetting Ltd,
Bury St Edmunds, Suffolk

Printed and bound in Great Britain by
Printed in Great Britain by Clays Ltd, St Ives plc

*shooting*fish

Prologue

Once upon a time there were two little boys who shared a dream. Their respective teachers regarded this dream with faint amusement and a tinge of pity. In fact, they regarded most of their charges' dreams with the same emotions. Not because these teachers were particularly unpleasant – although no one could have accused Miss Biggins of being downright pleasant. Miss Van der Pump, though, was reputed to be kind on a good day. Good days were Fridays when school finished early and she could bolt up to the Hamptons with her newly acquired (and thrillingly rich) significant other.

Miss Biggins, on the other hand (perhaps this was why

she was unpleasant?), lived in the East End of London, not in New York, and was not given to bolting anywhere. She did, grudgingly, take herself off to visit her mother in Bethnal Green on Fridays (when school finished early) but was not overly fond of so doing because her mother lived in a nursing home – an environment which reminded her of work, and of the boys with the Impossible Dreams. Or rather, the boy with the Impossible Dream.

'Now,' said Miss Biggins. (The 'now', strictly speaking, was a 'then'. This happened eighteen years ago.) 'Now,' she repeated to Simon, who, being thunderingly unimaginative, harboured no Impossible Dreams. 'Let's all have a look. Show the class where you'd most like to live when you grow up.'

As grubby and grey as his uniform, Simon held up a messy scrawl that Miss Biggins, being a veteran of such things, was able to identify as a pretty cottage, bordered by a picket fence and surrounded by trees and flowers. 'Good,' she said with a grimace, 'very good.' Privately, she thought it was appalling – but that wasn't why she was grimacing. In her book, boys who painted pretty rustic cottages were to be regarded with suspicion. As sure as eggs were eggs, they would, in the parlance used at St Mary's Orphanage of Tortured Souls, grow up with *Hellenic inclinations*. Miss Biggins held strong views on such matters.

She turned to a bright little girl called Anna. 'Now, Anna, what about you?'

Anna beamed and held up a picture of a giant boot with a chimney on the top. 'I want,' she said, 'to live in a big trainer.'

A strong adherent to the school of thought of *I want never gets*, Miss Biggins was sorely tempted to wallop Anna with, ideally, a big trainer. Then she looked more closely at the drawing. It was rather good. 'Oh, I see,' she said with a (real) smile, 'you want to be like the lady in the nursery rhyme. Like the old lady who lived in a shoe.' Though the old lady of legend didn't, suspected Miss Biggins, have NIKE emblazoned across her front porch. 'Very good, Anna. Now,' she said again, this time with a sigh as she turned to a boy sitting some way apart from the others, 'what about you . . . er . . . Jeremiah?'

Yes. What about Jeremiah Quinney.

Miss Biggins knew she shouldn't harbour such uncharitable thoughts, but she really wasn't surprised that Jeremiah had ended up in an orphanage. You could almost see a plaque above his head with the word MISFIT in large letters. Awkward and gangly, he had difficulty mixing with the other children – and the peculiar haircut didn't help. Nor did the fact that he seemed to live in his head, nurturing Impossible Dreams. At this moment, he had his back rudely turned away from Miss Biggins. 'Show us,' she urged in tones that harked back longingly to the days of corporal punishment, 'where you'd like to live when you're grown up.'

After a moment's hesitation, Jeremiah turned and, with some reluctance, reached beneath his desk. The other children gasped as he extracted an intricate, beautifully made construction of paper and card. No rosy cottage, this. No old boot. To Miss Biggins's utter amazement, it was a perfect replica of a Georgian stately home.

Miss Biggins wasn't sure whether to be admiring or cross. She opted for the middle ground. 'Er . . . where did you get this, Jeremiah?'

'Made it.'

Miss Biggins stepped closer and touched the masterpiece with a tentative finger. It even had pillars, she noted. Doric, she knew from her bus tours. Or possibly Ionic. Then again, they could be Corinthian . . .

'You made this,' she said, with what she suspected (and only half-regretted) was a snap, 'on your own?'

'Yes.' Jeremiah nodded his solemn head. 'It's where I want to live when I grow up. In a stately home.'

There was something rather unnerving about the boy's certainty, thought Miss Biggins. But it was simply too ridiculous for words to imagine that he had constructed this edifice all on his own. He was, after all, only eight. Dishonest little blighter.

'Well,' she said, 'it's lovely – but I'm sure someone must have helped you.' Miss Biggins leaned closer – all the better to fix the wretch with her beady, inquisitorial eye. 'Who made this, Jeremiah?'

Jeremiah didn't bat an eyelid. 'I did. And,' he added as he reached into the back of the house, 'I made the lights.'

To the amazement of everyone in the room, lights suddenly blazed from every window of the model.

Miss Biggins broke out into a sweat. 'But . . . how . . . ?'

'And,' interrupted Jeremiah, flicking another switch, 'I made the people.' There was, Miss Biggins would have noted, had she not been sweating uncomfortably, no boastfulness in his voice – he was simply stating facts. And the fact was that tiny paper figures inside the house were vibrating gently to and fro. The other children, now crowded round Jeremiah, began to cheer and, for the first time, Jeremiah seemed to derive pleasure from their company.

But Miss Biggins was beyond noticing such mundane matters. She was seriously beginning to question her sanity.

(Jeremiah's, as far as she was concerned, had always been open to question.) Paper houses constructed by eight-year-olds – Doric columns notwithstanding – should not light up and vibrate with life. Miss Biggins began to suspect extra-terrestrial interference.

'How,' she mumbled, 'did you . . . ?'

'I used the electric hole.' Jeremiah pointed to the wall behind him. To Miss Biggins's horror, she saw that the socket nearest to Jeremiah was primitively jammed with wires and bits of old cable.

She gaped, open-mouthed, at the sparks and blue flashes emanating from the hissing socket, then fainted dead away, depriving her pupils of their early Friday release from lessons and her mother of a dutiful visit. None of the deprived were unduly perturbed. The pupils were too caught up in Jeremiah's fabulous creation and the mother had always secretly found her one and only creation sadly wanting in the fabulous department and, anyway, preferred gin to visits. That Friday she drank a great deal of gin.

On the other side of the Atlantic, Miss Biggins's contemporary, Miss Van der Pump, had missed her appointment with her thrillingly rich boyfriend. And it was also the fault of an impudent eight-year-old.

Unlike Miss Biggins, Miss Van der Pump professed to adore all children. All children, that is, except Dylan Zimbler. She wasn't even convinced that Dylan *was* a child. There was something spookily adult about his conversation and attitude to life. The only pointer to childhood (Miss Van der Pump seemed to have forgotten Dylan's short stature and high voice) was his propensity to nurture Impossible Dreams. Of all the kids in the state orphanage, Dylan was the most prone to ridiculous notions. He was also the most troublesome, most wily and most confident child she had ever met. And, she reflected as she ran to the subway, he was the one most likely to end up in jail. At the moment, she actively wished him there. Were it not for Dylan, she would have been in time for her appointment. But for Dylan, she would not be obliged to take first the subway, then a train and then a bus to the Hamptons. Considering she was trying to masquerade as an extremely rich person, this was most ignominious. Her only consolation, as she darted underground to embark on the ignominy, was that Dylan's Impossible Dream had now turned into a Very Real Nightmare.

But not as far as Dylan was concerned. Back in the orphanage, he was having fun being interviewed by the principal of the orphanage and the man from the Internal Revenue Service.

'Now, Dylan,' sighed the principal, 'for the last time, I want you to tell the nice man from the IRS what you were doing in the bank this afternoon.'

Not for the first time, Dylan wondered if the principal, a Mr Knopf, was intellectually lacking. He turned his bright blue eyes on him and, trying his best not to sound patronizing, repeated his refrain, 'I told you, I was checking my account.'

'You're dyslexic,' snapped Mr Knopf.

'Yeah,' snapped Dylan, 'not innumerate.'

Mr Knopf took a deep breath. It would not do, he told himself, to be seen to be outsmarted by an eight-year-old — especially in the presence of this hatchet-faced individual from the IRS. 'Okay, Dylan,' he said with another sigh, 'we know that – but you don't *have* an account. You're not allowed to have an account. And,' he added, his voice rising, 'do you know *why* that is?'

Dylan knew why that was, but felt he ought to let Mr Knopf answer his own question. It was quite clear that the poor man was under stress and needed to let off steam.

Mr Knopf leaned towards Dylan. 'It's because,' he yelled, 'you're *eight*!'

This seemed a perfectly reasonable answer to Dylan. He nodded across the table. Mr Knopf stared back for a moment. This, he thought, is unbelievable. I am being made to look foolish by a kid. Then, foolishly, he lowered his head and banged it on the table in frustration.

The hatchet-faced man from the IRS was made of sterner stuff. He cast a pitying glance at the top of Mr Knopf's head and, from his position behind Dylan, barked a 'Let me handle this!' Then he grabbed the back of Dylan's chair. 'Now you little brat,' he snarled, 'we're all getting real tired here, so why don't you tell me, man to man, what was going on in the bank today?'

Dylan loathed being patronized – especially by someone with a personal hygiene problem. Still, he told himself, it would be best not to upset this individual. He had already – and not by design – reduced Miss Van der Pump to tears. And by the looks of things, Mr Knopf wasn't going to be too far behind. Dylan smiled up at the man from the IRS and then reached into his trouser pocket. 'I'm saving up,' he said as he handed over a crumpled piece of paper, 'for this.'

The man from the IRS uncrumpled the paper and spread it out on the table in front of Dylan. The action caused Mr Knopf to raise his head. Dylan noted that he was still dry-eyed. Then, in unison with the other man, he gasped as he looked at the picture on the paper. It was a copy of a photograph, a photograph of an extremely grand and exceedingly large English stately home. Blenheim Palace, he remembered from his British tour. Both men stared with wide-eyed incredulity at the vision in front of them. 'Jeez!' shouted the man from the IRS. 'Hell!'

Mr Knopf, while equally astonished, let slip the word 'Doric'. Or perhaps it was 'Ionic'. Dylan wasn't quite sure. Still, he was impressed. Imagine the principal knowing about Georgian porticoes.

'Dylan,' said Mr Knopf, displaying an unequal knowledge of Georgian prices, 'a mansion like that would cost you at least a hundred grand.'

The man from the IRS, who rather regretted the swearing, tried to make amends. 'Yah,' he sneered, in what he fondly imagined was an upper-class English voice rather than a Brooklyn twang, 'and how is an *orphan* – no offence – going to find that kind of money?'

Offence, of course, was clearly intended. It was not, however, easily taken.

'Easy.' Dylan beamed up at both men. 'Do a short strangle on the Hang Seng for a September expiry.'

Absolute and stunned silence greeted the remark. The man from the IRS looked at Mr Knopf. Mr Knopf looked at the man from the IRS. Both men looked at the picture of the stately home. Then they looked at Dylan.

Dylan was still beaming. 'I figure,' he said, indicating the picture, 'that I might have to wait till I'm older.'

'Oh, really?' The man from the IRS was recovering.

'Yeah. Say . . . eighteen years?'

Mr Knopf was looking covetously at the sandstone facade

surmounted by a grand cupola and flanked, he noted with approval, by symmetrical wings. He suspected there was a stable block in the background. Possibly even an orangery to the left. A great lake, he reckoned, would be lurking behind. Then he looked up, stunned, at the eight-year-old opposite him. 'A place like that'll cost a lot more in eighteen years.'

'Yeah,' said Dylan. 'I'm figuring on about two million.'

'Dollars?'

Dylan cast a pitying glance at his principal. 'No. Pounds.'

'And just how,' repeated the man from the IRS, 'is a kid like you going to raise that kinda dough?'

Dylan pondered that one for a moment and then looked at the hatchet-face in front of him. 'Well,' he said. 'That's for me to know – and you to find out.'

1

'Now,' said Dylan, addressing the table at large, 'do you know why you're here?'

Doubt suddenly registered on the faces of the eight men surrounding him. Of course they knew why they were here. They knew exactly why they had been invited. They were absolutely sure. They . . . they began to exchange uneasy glances. Something in the Yank's tone made them feel that the goal posts were about to be moved from under their feet.

'Mr Greenway,' Dylan turned to the man in his left, 'd'you know why you're here?'

'I –'

'You're here, Mr Greenway, to buy technology at its most advanced. You're here to buy a seventh generation computer. An HVRC system. A human voice recognition computer. A computer,' Dylan finished with a superb, imposing flourish, 'that talks to you.'

His words were met by absolute silence. It wasn't so much the words themselves that were so impressive, his audience reflected, but the person behind them. Tall, dark(ish) and imposing, he sported a perfect tan, perfect teeth and a perfectly tailored suit. He made the other men – all older than he – feel diminished in stature and importance. And he made Mr Greenway positively sick with envy. Pursing his gums round his dentures, he regretted his position as the senior IT buyer for Timpson's Travel and as spokesman for the group. He sat, short and stout in his chair, longing for someone else to say something, to divert attention from himself.

But no one else evinced a desire to utter a word. In thrall to the captivating, charismatic chairman of VerbaTec, it was all they could do to nod dumbly.

Dylan – in front of whom was a brass plate bearing the name DEKE WOLFORD – stood up suddenly and strode to the pin board at the end of the room. Unconsciously and in unison, the other men squared their shoulders.

'Are you at all familiar with the Symbleen mainframe computer?' Dylan asked. His penetrating eyes were firmly fixed on Mr Greenway, the others noted with relief.

'Um,' said the hapless buyer, wrestling with his dentures, 'a little.'

'Then you will know,' replied Dylan, theatrically ripping a photograph off the board and crumpling it into a ball, 'that it is a vastly expensive and, frankly, vastly overrated human voice recognition system. The Symbleen can understand three thousand common words, and has to be housed in an air-conditioned cabinet the size of this desk. Mr Greenway,' again the eyes flashed, 'it is completely useless – a scientist's toy.' With that, Dylan threw the crumpled photograph across the room. It landed squarely in the waste paper basket in the far corner, as everyone knew it would.

Dylan bestowed a dazzling smile on the room. Then, again, he turned to Mr Greenway. 'I'm going to keep things simple for you. Like,' he added, beaming with pride, 'our designers did on the VerbaTec VT 88-50 or,' he added with another, even broader smile, 'Johnson, as we call it.'

The other men smiled uneasily. Impressed to the point of intimidation, they couldn't wait for what would happen next.

'Gentlemen,' commanded Dylan as he sprang towards the door. 'Follow me!'

Without waiting to see if they would follow (people *always* followed Dylan), he swept into the corridor and opened the door opposite the boardroom. This room, somewhat to the surprise of the men snaking in behind him, was empty, apart from a short table on which sat a small desktop computer and a sleek, matt-black box. If Mr Greenway hadn't been so knowledgeable and desperately important in the computer world he would have thought the black box was a video recorder.

'This,' said Dylan, in the manner of a proud father introducing his first-born son, 'is Johnson.' He patted the black box with an exquisitely manicured hand. 'The very first computer to be truly free of a keyboard. Mr Greenway,' he continued with another beguiling smile, 'no one likes to type; everyone likes to talk. I like to talk,' he said with a self-deprecating laugh, 'you like to talk.' (This, of course, wasn't strictly true, but Dylan wasn't quite up to speed with Mr Greenway's orthodontic arrangements.) 'Johnson here,' he added, patting the box again, 'doesn't just understand three thousand words, nor just six thousand words – your or my common vocabulary.' (This wasn't true, either. Mr Greenway's vocabulary was almost as limited as his intelligence, while Dylan's far exceeded that of most mortals.)

'Mr Greenway: secretaries are going to hate this machine.' This was absolutely the right thing to say. Mr Greenway hated secretaries and couldn't wait to dispense with every single one who had ever darkened the door of his company. 'Johnson understands eighty thousand and twenty-four words; he will type, file, word process, do your accounts.' Dylan could read people like a book and Greenway was easily digested. The slight sheen on his forehead and the unattractive panting indicated that the scything of secretaries was high on his list of priorities. 'He will, in short, put your secretary out of a job. The only thing you'll have to do is buy your wife's birthday present – and Johnson will remind you of the date. And,' added Dylan, unable to stop himself, 'if she's not your wife . . .' He accompanied the unfinished sentence with a teasing twinkle in his eye before realizing, too late, that Mr Greenway was highly unamused. Indeed, he looked extremely uncomfortable.

'Enough,' said Dylan with a short laugh, 'of this chitter-chatter. Let's see this baby work. Johnson,' he said, addressing the black box, 'good afternoon.'

The moment of truth had arrived. For one horrible moment Dylan thought that Johnson might continue his impersonation of a deceased video recorder and remain mute.

He didn't. Instead a spookily soulless yet loud and distinct voice reverberated around the room. 'Good afternoon, Wolford.' Simultaneously, those same words appeared on the computer monitor.

'Great, huh?' Dylan turned, grinning, to his audience. 'But I can tell you're dying to try him out for yourself. So,' he continued, gesturing for Greenway to step forward, 'I'm going to introduce you to Johnson. Johnson,' he said, turning back to the computer, 'key, introducing Greenway.'

'Welcome, Greenway,' said Johnson. 'Please speak to me.'

Not many people extended such an invitation to Greenway. Visibly excited, he stepped forward.

'We need a voice recognition sequence,' interjected Dylan. 'Try "I'm a Little Teapot".'

'What?' Greenway looked extremely alarmed.

'The nursery rhyme. It contains all the vowel sounds Johnson needs.'

'Oh . . . right . . . er . . .' Feeling self-conscious and not a little foolish, Greenway faltered and then, after a deep breath, began, 'I'm a little teapot . . .'

Nodding enthusiastically, Dylan prompted him on. 'Good . . . short and stout . . .'

'. . . short and stout . . .' Greenway was beginning to get into the swing of things. The words were flowing more easily. Behind him, his colleagues were having difficulty controlling themselves.

'Where's your handle . . . ?' encouraged Dylan.

'Here's my handle . . .' warbled Greenway, patting his hip.

'And . . . ?'

'And here's my spout!' Greenway's left hand waved around at a camp angle above his head.

'Spout,' repeated Johnson. 'Voice recognition complete. Thank you, Greenway.'

'That,' said Greenway, as he peered at Johnson, 'is remarkable.'

Dylan smiled an inscrutable smile. 'But you are thinking that Timpson's Travel already has computers. How, you are asking yourself, will one Johnson fit in – let alone the ten machines you require?'

Mr Greenway hadn't been aware of needing ten Johnsons. Yet, if he had ten Johnsons, Timpson's would be at the cutting edge of the travel industry. Not, of course, that it wasn't already . . .

'That,' Mr Greenway repeated, 'is incredible.' He turned, smiling broadly – a dangerous activity, considering the dentures' propensity to bolt for freedom – at his colleagues. They, too, were grinning and nodding at Dylan. The whole process had been incredible. Remarkable. They were nodding like automatons.

Dylan knew he had them all in the palm of his hand. Soon, he would have something else in that palm.

Sooner than he thought. 'What,' asked Greenway, 'is your finance deal on these things?'

Dylan adopted the half-embarrassed, half-apologetic expression he used for discussing finance with the English. 'Well, sir . . . as you can imagine, orders are flowing in.' Then, bowing his head slightly in deference to the great Greenway, he took a deep breath. 'A deposit of ten per cent,' he finished, 'would secure a guaranteed delivery of the ten machines you need.'

'Marvellous!' Greenway turned to the man on his left. 'Skippings – the chequebook.'

Skippings, too, bowed his head. Not in deference to Greenway, but simply out of habit. Every time his name was mentioned, he recoiled slightly, as if trying to dissociate himself from the word *Skippings*. People sympathized.

But Dylan wasn't interested in Skippings's head-bowing activities. He was interested in the man's right hand as it extracted a chequebook from his breast pocket and, with a reluctance born of the fact that he was going to have to write the wretched word as well as hear it, penned his signature. Dylan attributed the reluctance to the amount Skippings was obliged to 'pay bearer' and wasn't, frankly, surprised. To his mind it was completely outrageous. Then, looking suddenly relieved, Skippings handed the cheque to Greenway.

Holding a large cheque in his hand gave Greenway almost as much of a kick as contemplating the imminent redundancy of his secretary. He smiled importantly, and glared at his colleagues to do likewise. They obeyed, as they seemed to do everything else, in perfect unison. Timpson's Travel was clearly not a place for the adventurous or independent spirit. Group outings, thought Dylan, were evidently their thing.

Then Greenway handed the cheque over. 'Mr Wolford, it has been a pleasure doing business with you.'

You'll be wanting to alter that statement shortly, thought Dylan, as he smiled his dazzling smile and extended his hand. 'Deke, Mr Greenway,' he urged as he clasped the other man's puffy little hand. 'Call me Deke.'

And then the team from Timpson's Travel trotted out towards, if they but knew it, imminent redundancy. Dylan consoled himself with the happy thought that they would at least be together on the firing range, that they would be glad to be sacked simultaneously. The ultimate group outing, he supposed.

Then, smiling to himself, Dylan reached to his left ear and extracted a tiny earphone. Breathing a sigh of elation mixed with sudden exhaustion, he walked back towards Johnson, towards the magical black box, the great VerbaTec VT.

With a wicked grin, Dylan lifted the cover . . . revealing the inner secrets of the seventh generation of computers. They were, in descending order of expense: a speaker, a radio microphone and a brick.

Dylan leaned towards the microphone and yelled at the top of his voice: 'We did it!'

Because his earphone was in his hand and not in his ear, he could barely hear the succinct reply indicating a burst eardrum at the other end. 'Bastard!' came a feeble squawk from the earpiece. Dylan grinned.

Had a certain Miss Biggins been in the room and not, as was the case, incarcerated in a Home for the Bewildered, she would not have grinned. She would have scowled. She might even have screamed. And she would certainly have been transported back some eighteen years to a classroom in the East End. The voice, for all that it was deeper and less harsh, was unmistakably that of Jeremiah Quinney.

2

So the Impossible Dreams of two little boys came true?

Well . . . no. Not yet. Not, in fact, even nearly yet. But Jeremiah (now Jez) and Dylan had at least taken one step towards realizing their dreams. They had met each other.

They actually met in a gasometer (more of which later) and cemented an instant, intense friendship. Not of the dodgy sort, but of the kindred spirit variety. Both, they discovered, had been orphaned at an obscenely early age. Both had found it difficult to fit into society (Jez was still awkward and Dylan was, after all, still American). They were both poor: Jez's poverty being due to an inability to hold down a job, Dylan's to an allergy to normal work.

On the upside, they discovered that they shared the same ambitions. One of these was fairly straightforward: to live in an exceptionally large and exceedingly beautiful stately home. The other was more complex. It involved becoming thrillingly rich (remember Miss Van der Pump's Significant Other? Miss Van der Pump prefers not to. The man in question belongs to the Once Upon a Time category. Not, most emphatically not, to the Happily Ever After one) without working and without spending any money. The never spending any money bit had been a doddle. So had the not working. The thrillingly rich aspect had, as yet, eluded them. Yet they still entertained high hopes.

Dylan was better at high hopes than Jez. He had carried them with him throughout the length and breadth of the United States after leaving the orphanage at the age of sixteen. Yet despite Dylan's ingenuity, his good looks, his articulacy and his intelligence, he had never quite found what his mother (had he had one) would have called his *niche*. The Internal Revenue Service would have begged to differ and, having identified one Dylan Zimbler – under various aliases – as the perpetrator of some of the most outrageous cons ever undertaken in thirty-five of America's fifty states, had pursued him with a vengeance. They found themselves accompanied by the FBI, the CIA, the DEA, the RGD, the YOA, the PTA and the XYZ. Sensibly concluding that his luck had run out, Dylan decided to leave the country. He headed, via Canada, Greenland, several aliases, Ireland and Scotland for London. Thence to the gasometer (more of which etc.) and the meeting with Jez.

Jez, meanwhile, had been leading a quiet life in London. Like Dylan, he had emerged from his institution at the age of sixteen and, unlike Dylan, had the benefit of state funding to help him find a job. Not that America was lacking in any desire to help its less fortunate citizens. It was more that Dylan, having fallen foul of the IRS at an early age (remember Hatchet-Face? Nobody else does. He committed suicide after a disastrous short strangle on the Hang Seng for a September expiry), had been deemed less than fortunate and beyond redemption and therefore ill-qualified for benefit.

Jez was more favoured. Given that his unfortunate haircut and awkward manner had stayed with him longer than Miss Biggins (and we know what happened to her), he was given all manner of grants. But despite the granting he remained unemployable and unemployed. Technically brilliant on the one hand, he was terminally unemployable on the other.

But Jez's past can wait. We don't want to lose interest in his present activities which, after Dylan's yell down the microphone, consisted mainly of rubbing his sore ear.

'Are you all right?' asked Georgie with genuine concern. Georgie was the secretary Dylan had employed for the duration of the InfoTec scam. For, that is, one day.

Jez looked up and smiled. 'Fine,' he said with a rueful grin. From the moment he had clapped eyes on her, Jez had felt rueful. Georgie was stunning. Precisely the sort of girl that an awkward grown-up orphan with a permanently bad haircut would never be able to date. Still, she was spirited and nice to him. (Girls had, in Jez's past, tended to be dispirited and not at all nice to him.)

'How,' added Jez with, this time, a sympathetic smile, 'are the fingers?'

Now it was Georgie who looked rueful. 'Sore.' As she spoke, she massaged one hand with the other and looked with distaste at the keyboard in front of her. Beside the keyboard lay a set of discarded headphones – the other 'missing' parts of Johnson's equipment. While Jez had been his voice, Georgie had been his keyboard, frantically typing out verses of 'I'm a Little Teapot' in time with Mr Greenway's delighted, if off-key, rendition.

Then Dylan burst in from the next-door office. As ever, he was accompanied by high-voltage energy and a dazzling smile. 'Yes!' he yelled, punching the air. Then he grabbed Jez, sweeping him up in his enthusiasm and consigning the sore ear to history. They danced around the little unfurnished room, whooping with delight. Georgie looked on, a bemused and increasingly suspicious expression darkening her beautiful features. She had her doubts about Jez and Dylan. Severe doubts.

Then Dylan noticed her, abandoned Jez and swept her into his arms. They made, Jez couldn't help noticing, a beautiful couple, as they jigged around the room.

Dylan beamed at Georgie. 'Fantastic finger work . . . er . . .' The beautiful moment had gone. He'd forgotten her name.

'Georgie.' The cut-glass vowels echoed coldly through the room. Then Georgie pulled away from Dylan and shot him a sarcastic look. 'I can't begin to tell you what that means to me.'

But her words were wasted on Dylan. He was still high as a kite over the success of his mission. 'This is going so well. Really well. Relax,' he said, looking from Georgie to Jez. 'You can both take five.'

But Georgie was beginning to harbour ideas about taking her leave. 'Before we carry on,' she said, 'can I ask you something?'

'Sure. Shoot.'

Georgie fixed Dylan with a penetrating glare. 'You are sure this is all above board, aren't you?'

Behind her, Jez froze. This was precisely the sort of question that threw him into a blind panic. Precisely the sort of question that had led, in the past, to the failure of many of his missions.

But Dylan, being Dylan, was completely unfazed by the question. And having just fleeced a troupe of hardened businessmen, he wasn't going to have any difficulty placating an uppity secretary. Particularly one wearing, he noted with distaste, clumpy Doc Martens. 'Look,' he said with one of his ready smiles. 'There's nothing for you to worry about.' He gestured expansively round the office. 'It's all completely . . . completely as it looks.'

It looked, thought Jez, well dodgy.

'Didn't I explain it properly to you before?' finished Dylan with wide-eyed innocence.

'No. You didn't, actually.'

'Well.' Dylan walked to the window. 'It works like this. You see . . . Ah!'

'What?'

As he looked out of the window, Dylan could see that the next group of potential buyers had arrived. He had no time to waste. Time was money. Time was, to be precise, the one day that this suite of offices would be empty before the next, real tenants moved in.

'Gotta go,' said Dylan, rushing to the door. Then he turned back to Georgie. 'I'll talk to you later. I promise.'

'But . . .'

But Dylan had lost interest in his uppity secretary. 'Quick,' he said to Jez, 'give me another photo.'

Jez handed his friend a copy of the photograph that Dylan had thrown in the boardroom bin. 'Oh, and Dylan,' Jez said, as he handed it over, 'it's a sixth generation computer. Not seventh.'

'Sure, sure. Okay, guys – let's get back to work.' As he opened the door, Dylan cast a final, encouraging look at a distinctly mutinous-looking Georgie. 'Georgie, Georgie, Georgie . . . don't worry! We're good guys, I promise. Just trust me, okay?' *Trust me* was a phrase that tripped often from Dylan's tongue. Despite endless repetition, it still carried conviction. Or perhaps, thought Georgie, as she succumbed and reached for her headphones, it was the innocent look in those wonderful clear blue eyes that did the trick. 'God,' she said to herself as she sat at the keyboard and donned the phones. 'I need this like . . .' And then she remembered. 'Like I need the money.'

Georgie, then, had at least one thing in common with Jez and Dylan. Her quest for money, however, was more noble than theirs, although her methods of obtaining it were less grandiose and ambitious. She had found her present employment by placing an advertisement in a newsagent's window. It had read No JOB TOO BIG, TOO SMALL OR TOO DIFFICULT – precisely the sort of words guaranteed to appeal, had she but known it, to Dylan.

Yet as Georgie readdressed herself to typing the lines of 'I'm a Little Teapot' all over again at Dylan's cue from the next room, she reflected that this particular job was either too big, too small, or too difficult – or possibly all three. These two characters, she decided, were small-time crooks engaged in a big-time scam and, while they seemed to have no difficulty in extracting vast sums of money from their 'clients', Georgie suspected that they had their own, idiosyncratic notions about the Theory of Reciprocity. She suspected – and was becoming increasingly positive – that, to them, *give and take* meant that everyone else gave whilst they took. And as far as Georgie was concerned, this would mean that she would give her services and they would give her no money in return.

These thoughts continued to plague Georgie as the day wore unexcitingly on. Why, she said to herself as, for the umpteenth time, she typed the words 'short and stout', was she doing this? Why, as she banged out 'here's my spout', didn't she just run out? She was getting herself involved, she mused as she tapped the word 'handle', in a terrible scandal. Why waste her prime on silly rhymes?

Then Georgie realized that insanity was beckoning. Most poets (although they didn't know it) drove themselves mad and she, Georgie, was teetering on the edge of the abyss of dementia because she couldn't find a word to rhyme with 'teapot'. It simply wouldn't do.

'I'm leaving,' she said, suddenly standing up and taking off her headphones.

Opposite her, Jez went white. In the next room, Dylan had just ushered in the last customer of the day and, as Georgie's words came through his earpiece, uttered a frenzied 'No!' in response to that customer's *Isn't it a lovely afternoon?*

Things were not looking good.

'Please,' implored Jez. 'You can't.'

Stomping towards him in her DMs, Georgie held out her hand. 'I want my money.'

'But . . . but . . .' Jez cast frantically around. He needed Dylan for this. But then Dylan needed him. And, particularly, Georgie. Then Jez saw Georgie's newsagent's card lying on the floor beside him. 'But look,' he pleaded. 'Here's your advertisement. It says . . .'

'Give me that card a second.' Snatching it from Jez's trembling hand, Georgie scanned it with her most supercilious expression. 'Nope,' she said at length. 'Can't seem to find "No job too dodgy". See ya.' With that, she turned towards the door.

But there was a barrier between Georgie and the door – Jez. Unable to think of anything else to do, he threw himself on his knees at her feet, blocking her path and looking up at her with a desperate, beseeching face. Despite the ridiculous pose and the hideous haircut, Georgie thought he looked rather sweet. But she was still determined to leave.

In the next room, Dylan was beginning to panic. He had apologized for his strange greeting, attributing it (truthfully) to a sudden and exceedingly sharp pain in his ear. Then he had agreed (untruthfully) that it was a lovely afternoon. His afternoon had turned suddenly horrible.

But Mrs Ross, the last customer of the day, was still standing at the threshold of the boardroom. Smartly dressed in a suit almost as well-cut as Dylan's and with an air of confidence to match, she was clearly not the sort of lady accustomed to standing on boardroom thresholds chatting about earaches and the weather.

'Can I come in?'

At the same time, through the earpiece, came Georgie's 'Let me out!'

'What?' barked Dylan.

Mrs Ross recoiled in horror.

'Oh, I'm *terribly* sorry,' gushed Dylan, recovering with admirable speed. 'I was actually expecting . . . ahh . . .

where's your team?' An audience of one was, in his experience, much more difficult to mesmerize. Especially one such as Mrs Ross. She looked distinctly formidable.

She was. She brushed past Dylan with a smile that failed to reach her eyes and the words, 'It's probably easier if you just talk to me, isn't it?'

'Absolutely,' said Dylan wondering, as Georgie had done earlier, if he was about to lose his sanity. He followed Mrs Ross into the boardroom, ushered her into a chair and prepared to launch into his sales pitch.

In his left ear, Georgie was pitching her own ideas. 'I mean,' he heard her say, 'I don't want to be rude, but you're con men, aren't you?'

'In many ways,' replied the still-supplicant Jez, 'no.'

'What are you then?'

'Well ... we're ... we're actually the Robin Hoods of the nineties.'

And I, thought Georgie, am Friar Tuck. 'What,' she demanded, 'does that mean?'

'It means we ... we, er, rob the rich to feed the poor.'

'Oh, yes. And that's what Robin Hood did?' Georgie knew her history. Not for her the myths about men in tights.

'It's what *we* do,' replied Jez, warming to his theme. 'All the money we get is going to the poor people.' He looked imploringly at Georgie. 'Scout's honour.'

'Scout's haircut,' snorted Georgie.

Next door, Dylan was finding it impossible to devote his attentions to Mrs Ross. The earpiece would have to go. With what he hoped was a subtle, swift movement of the earache-alleviating variety, he snatched it out and deposited it in his pocket. Then he beamed at the frowning lady opposite. 'Mrs Ross,' he began, 'do you know why you are here?'

But Mrs Ross was no Mr Greenway, no nodding dog from Timpson's Travel. Dylan thought it best to press swiftly on. 'You are here,' he contintued, 'to see technology at its most advanced, You are here –'

'Cut the hard sell, Mr Wolford. If the machine works, I'll buy it. In fact, I'll buy your company.'

Dylan's ears went pink. 'Absolutely, Mrs Ross.' He stood up and gestured towards the door. 'Follow me.' Hyperventilating, Dylan shot into the opposite room and cast a baleful look at Johnson. This should have been it: the greatest sale of his life, his greatest chance. But how, without the support of his colleagues, could he possibly persuade Mrs Ross to buy a company that consisted of nothing more than a black box, a speaker, a microphone and a brick?

'Is that it?' said Mrs Ross, looking at Johnson.

'Yes. Very . . . very space-saving, don't you think?'

It wasn't entirely clear from Mrs Ross's expression exactly what she did think. Was that doubt he could read on her face? Or awe?

'First,' continued the desperate Dylan, 'we have to do the voice recognition sequence but . . . er, before that –'

'What platform is it?'

'What?'

'Platform,' repeated Mrs Ross.

'Platform?'

'Yes. Platform.'

'D'ya know,' said Dylan, looking at his watch, 'I think our engineer is due back from the factory any time now. Why don't you ask him?'

'But I just want to see it run the . . .'

But Dylan was already wrenching at the door. The game was up. There would be no more stalling Mrs Ross. There was, however, the not entirely unattractive notion of locking her in the room until he and his bickering colleagues had scarpered. That, then, was the new plan.

Until Jez ruined it. When Dylan threw open the door, it revealed a dishevelled and unhappy looking Jez, gibbering about Georgie, threats, scouts, haircuts and money. Money, most of all. Georgie's money.

Dylan looked at him, open-mouthed with horror. Plan B had just been blown away, to be replaced by . . .

Plan A again.

Dylan was nothing if not quick off the mark. Jez looked like the archetypal computer engineer; Jez *was* the archetypal computer engineer. He was strange-looking, he had an appalling haircut, he was wearing flared jeans and he was socially incompetent. Perfect.

Dylan grabbed his gibbering colleague by the lapels of his white lab coat and hauled him into the room. 'This,' he said with the air of one who has just saved a rare species from extinction, 'is VerbaTec. Otherwise known as . . . as Hepworth.'

Mrs Ross looked at the rare species.

'He is,' said Dylan in a stage whisper, 'a little strange. Now,' he added to Jez, 'Mrs Ross wants to know about the plateau.'

'Plateau?' Jez was in total confusion. Everything was happening too quickly. And he wasn't even sure what everything was.

'Platform,' corrected Dylan. 'And this is Mrs Ross. I'm afraid,' he added, 'that I've got to make a few calls.' Without giving either of them a chance to reply, he shot out of the room and slammed the door behind him.

Jez looked at Mrs Ross. Mrs Ross looked at Jez. They looked straight into each other's eyes.

In films – particularly black and white ones – this would be the moment when our heroic couple, say, Lana Turner and Clark Gable, know that they're going to live Happily Ever After. Their eyes lock together and they just know that there are only a few scenes to go before they dash off to Lana's mansion; before Clark gets fresh; before Lana swoons and whispers the immortal line, 'Oops, there goes my ballgown.'

This, however, was not a black and white movie. Mrs Ross, while passably attractive, could not have been mistaken for Lana Turner. She possessed neither mansion nor ballgown. And Jez had absolutely nothing of the Clark Gable about him. True, he was quivering – but with nerves rather than lust.

'Platform?' prompted Mrs Ross – rather in the manner that Lana may have offered 'drink?'.

'UNIX,' replied Jez.

Mrs Ross sighed with pleasure.

'Actually,' said Jez, suddenly more confident, 'it's a beta version of UNIX NT.'

Lana Turner would have been flummoxed. Not Mrs Ross. Her eyebrows shot upwards. 'Advanced OS. Impressive. Can it make format view files?'

'Yes.' Jez started quivering again. It could make format view files – but only if Dylan had had the intelligence to nip next door, don the headphones and . . . and learn something about computers.

*   *   *

36

'Format view files,' said Dylan in a desperate whisper. 'What is it?'

Georgie stared at him. She had been expecting Jez to return with her money. Dylan bounding in and taking over Jez's position had not been on the agenda. And now, like Jez, he was imploring her to help him. 'What,' she said after moment of frosty silence, 'do you do with the money?'

'What?' Dylan was only half listening. He had found a computer manual and, a stranger to such publications, was holding it upside down, searching frantically for format files.

'How,' repeated Georgie, 'do you spend the money?'

Next door, and via Dylan's earpiece, Mrs Ross was trying to log into Johnson. Beside her, Jez was quivering.

'Come on,' snarled Georgie, 'what do you spend it on? Fast cars? Women?' Then, looking at Dylan's bronzed complexion, she sneered, 'Sunbeds?'

Dylan looked up with pleading eyes and held out the manual. At the same time, Mrs Ross repeated her request to set up a format view file. Heart pounding, Dylan spoke into his mike, 'Do not recognize format view file. Searching data bank for possible match.'

In the room next door, his words came out – thanks to the distortion of the brick – in Johnson's voice, but with an American twang. Mrs Ross seemed, if not altogether satisfied, at least convinced. Beside her, Jez allowed himself a small sigh of relief.

But Dylan knew he had only bought a few seconds. 'Please, Georgie,' he urged, 'you've got to help me. I'm alphabetically illiterate.'

In response, Georgie picked up her bag. 'What,' she sighed, 'do you spend the money on?'

'The money?'

'The money.'

'Ah. The money. The money. We . . . we give it to . . . to orphans.' Brilliant! thought Dylan. What a flash of inspiration.

'Orphans?'

Dylan peered at Georgie. She was, he reckoned, beginning to waver. 'Yes. An orphans' housing project.' He looked away and lowered his voice. 'For those poor children without parents.'

No reply from Georgie. Then, just as Dylan thought he had blown it, she dropped her bag on the floor. 'Okay,' she said, 'give me the manual.'

Dylan allowed himself a long sigh of relief.

A moment later, Mrs Ross's screen filled with coloured graphics and the words FORMAT FILE flashed in front of her.

'Match correct?' boomed Johnson.

'That,' said a delighted Mrs Ross, 'is amazing.' She turned and beamed at Jez. Her beam faltered somewhat when she noticed the two enormous – and growing – patches of sweat under his I BUILT VERBATEC T-shirt. It wasn't, she thought, even remotely warm in the room. And then she remembered that Jez was a computer engineer. Personal hygiene problems were, of course, endemic in the species.

Jez nodded down at her. Any minute now, he told himself, this will be over and I can relax.

Then Mrs Ross reached forward and picked up the black box. 'Can I have a look inside? I'd be really interested in the circuit layout.'

This, thought Jez, is not happening to me. I want out of

here. I want to disappear. I want to die. I'll gladly go to hell. I'll pray for anything, everything, anybody. Even Miss Biggins.

'Um . . .' he said. 'Well, I think . . . I think . . .'

'Bullshit her!' commanded Dylan through his earpiece.

'What?' replied a startled Jez.

'What?' Mrs Ross had thought her question perfectly clear.

'Bullshit her,' urged Dylan again. 'You told me the thing would work in theory.'

'It does work,' Jez was indignant. 'In theory.'

Mrs Ross looked up in suspicion. 'What do you mean, *in theory*?'

'In theory,' replied Jez, for the benefit of both visible and invisible audiences, 'it has always worked. But now . . . now it's here, in practice . . . working.' He turned to Mrs Ross and mustered a smile. 'Let me just draw you a diagram.' Without giving her a chance to object, he ripped down a poster from the wall, pulled a pen from his back pocket and started to scribble madly.

Mrs Ross wasn't quite sure how to react, especially when Jez's diagram became increasingly complex, requiring several posters and, in order to view it, both of them to squat on the floor. Mrs Ross wasn't overly fond of squatting, nor, as the diagram grew, of lying on floors. On the other hand, she was madly keen to know everything there was to know about VerbaTec, and she didn't want to offend this strange young man. The species, she knew, was generally placid but was also easily roused to anger.

It was not the man himself but the patches of sweat that finally got to her. 'Please,' she said as, camel-like, she lumbered to her feet. 'It really would be easier if I could see the circuitry itself.' To prove how easy it would be, she delved into her handbag and extracted a penknife.

Oh floor, prayed Jez, swallow me up.

'Oh, God,' said Dylan next door.

'What?'

'The box, Georgie. She's trying to open the box.'

'Pandora's box?'

'Whaddya mean?' Dylan's education, whilst broad, hadn't extended to the classics. Classic scams, maybe – but not classic literature.

'Pandora,' explained Georgie, 'was a lady with a box.'

'Like Mrs Ross?'

'Is that her name?'

'Whose name?' Dylan was becoming confused.

'Mrs Ross's,' frowned Georgie. Then, after a pause, 'How did you know her name was Pandora?'

'You told me.'

'No I didn't.'

'You did too.'

'I did not.'

'You did.'

'Did I?' Georgie, too, was becoming confused. 'Well, that makes it even more appropriate then.'

'Why?'

'Because Pandora wasn't allowed to open the box –'

'Like Mrs Ross.'

'– but she disobeyed and let loose all the evils in the world.'

'Not like Mrs Ross, then. The box she has contains a speaker, a microphone and a brick. Oh God,' finished Dylan as screwdriving sounds filtered through his earpiece, 'she's opening it!'

'– and when she closed it,' continued Georgie, pleased with her powers of recall, 'she trapped something really important inside.'

'And what was that?' Dylan didn't really care what it was. Still, it might provide a clue about how to get out of this mess.

'Hope,' replied Georgie.

For the second time that day, Dylan began to hyperventilate.

'Are you all right?' asked Georgie in genuine concern as she saw him fighting for breath.

'Yeah,' gasped Dylan, 'I'm cool. It's Jez who has the trouble with pressure, not me.'

Georgie leaped to her feet. 'Paper bag,' she said, looking around.

'What?' rasped Dylan.

'Paper bag. Where would I find one?'

'In . . . in . . . the . . . bin.' Dylan had turned blue.

Moving with brisk efficiency, Georgie upturned the bin, found a paper bag and, putting it to her mouth, inflated it. Then she placed it over Dylan's mouth. 'Breathe into this steadily,' she commanded.

Dylan did as he was told.

'And now,' said Georgie, as the colour began to return to Dylan's face, 'I've really got to go.'

'But . . .'

But Georgie didn't go immediately. Not, that is, out of the building. Instead she dashed into the next door office.

She arrived just in the nick of time. Mrs Ross, as handy with a screwdriver as she was with everything else, was on the last screw. Jez, Georgie noted with alarm, appeared to be trying to crawl through the floor.

41

Adopting her best bored and bolshy secretary stance, Georgie leaned against the doorframe and stared with glacial disinterest into the middle of the room. 'Anyone here own a red Audi?' she drawled.

'Yes,' said Mrs Ross. 'Why?'

'It's about to get clamped.'

Mrs Ross was from good, God-fearing Calvinist stock. While willing to spend a fortune on a potentially lucrative computer company, she was damned if she was going to waste well-earned money recovering her car from the pound. She shot out of the room and out of the building.

When she returned, there was no trace of Dylan, Georgie or the endangered species. Nor was there any sign of the black box or the computer monitor. The demonstration room was empty apart from Jez's laboriously drawn – and highly accurate – diagram. And a brick. Mrs Ross was bemused, though not distraught. Computer people, she knew, were prone to strange behaviour. And she wouldn't, anyway, leave empty-handed. She bent down and picked up the various sheets of paper that constituted the diagram and bundled them into her briefcase. She hurried into the office next door. It, too, was empty – apart from a small newsagent's card and a warm paper bag. She ignored the latter but picked up the former. It bore the legend No JOB TOO BIG, TOO SMALL OR TOO DIFFICULT. Below that was an address. Smiling to herself, Mrs Ross slipped the card into her breast pocket and left the premises.

Seven cars in front of her as she drove through London on her way home, an elderly Rover 90 belched its way through the traffic. In it were two men and a girl – and on the rear windscreen was a sticker bearing the legend I LOVE BLENHEIM PALACE.

3

'That,' said Jez, 'was wonderful, Georgie.'

'Could I have my cheque now, please?'

'Your cheque?' In the front passenger seat, Dylan turned round and grinned at Georgie. 'Did I ask you this before? Have you done some modelling?'

Georgie raised her eyebrows. 'You did, yes.'

But Dylan was on a high and wasn't in the mood for discussing the piffling amounts of money he had promised Georgie. Not when they had just made the decidedly unpiffling amount of one hundred thousand pounds. 'Can you believe it back there?' he said to Jez. 'It was like shooting fish.'

'Shooting fish?'

'Yeah. In a barrel.'

Jez frowned. The language barrier, even after five years, hadn't quite been demolished. 'What's that mean?'

'Uh . . . well . . .' This time Dylan frowned. The words *swindle, defraud, rip-off with ease* seemed so crass. Especially in front of a nice girl like Georgie.

'It means,' piped up Georgie from behind them, 'that it's really easy to rip people off. To swindle and defraud them. Easy and fun.'

'Wasn't that easy,' objected a miffed Dylan. 'We put a lot of work into that operation.'

'When I told her,' said Jez, remembering Mrs Ross, 'that the CPU had a built-in sound byte interface she didn't even blink.'

'Wow.' Dylan flicked through the cheques in his hand. 'We are so close. One more and I think we're there.'

'Can I have my cheque now, please?'

'Georgie, Georgie, Georgie! Bear with us. We have to go to the bank first.'

Georgie thought this boded well.

It didn't. Ten minutes later, Jez screeched to a halt outside a bank. Hand on the door handle, Dylan turned before leaping out of the car. 'We'll just get these cleared and then close the InfoTec account, yeah?'

'Yeah.'

'And come back in three days to pick up the balance.'

'In cash.'

'In cash.'

'Can I,' said Georgie, 'have my money in cash as well, please?'

But Dylan had already left the car.

44

Georgie leaned forward. 'Is he always like this?'

'Like what?'

'Manic.'

Jez pondered that one for a moment. 'Well, he *is* American.'

'How did you two meet?'

Again Jez pondered. Whilst the correct reply would have been 'in a gasometer', he assumed (rightly) that Georgie would take this as an indication that both he and Dylan were even stranger than she had initially assumed. And he didn't want Georgie to think him too strange. He wanted Georgie to like him. He liked Georgie. He liked being with Georgie – but he didn't like her breathing down his neck. It made him feel hot under the collar.

He turned round and smiled at her. 'Let's wait for Dylan outside the bank.'

'We are outside the bank.'

'No, but *right* outside the bank. That way you . . . er, can be sure of getting your money.'

'Don't you trust Dylan?'

'I'd trust him,' said Jez, 'with my life.'

Georgie knew he meant it. There was something rather touching about the relationship between these two, a sort of *us against the world* mentality. It was, she thought, really rather sweet.

Then she remembered that they owed her money and shot out of the car.

Jez followed her.

Dylan was emerging from the bank as they reached the entrance. Without a word, Georgie held out a hand.

Dylan grinned and reached for his wallet. 'Yeah, okay. Fifty bucks.'

Georgie shook her head. 'One hundred and fifty pounds.'

Dylan reeled back in horror. 'Seventy-five quiddos now and we give you the rest, cash, on Friday. That is quite normal for secretarial work, honey.'

'It's weird,' said Georgie, with an inscrutable smile, 'but *normal* wasn't quite the word that sprung to mind during the course of my employment with you. Maybe,' she added, 'I should ask the gentlemen who invested all that money in VerbaTec today if they think it's normal?'

Dylan was momentarily lost for words. Then, looking piqued, he shook his head. 'Y'know, that kind of attitude is so uncharitable. Did Live Aid mean nothing?'

By rights, thought Georgie, this man should be insufferable. Unscrupulous, immoral and impossible – yet somehow he was likeable. It really shouldn't be allowed. She turned to Jez. He grinned back.

God, thought Georgie. Peas in a pod. She let out a long, weary sigh – and then a scream.

'What?' Startled out of their wits, Jez and Dylan gawped at her. Georgie didn't appear to be the screaming type.

'The car!' she screamed again, pointing to the Rover.

Both men whirled round. As they did so, the rear window of the Rover shattered, a hand poked through and, a second later, emerged from the car with Jez's laptop and Georgie's handbag. Then the hand ran away. Not, of course, of its own volition, but because it was attached to a body and therefore the legs of a brutish-looking individual.

'No!' shouted Jez.

'Shit!' from Dylan.

'My bag!' wailed Georgie. 'My notes are in it!'

They gave chase. But the brutish-looking individual was evidently not as stupid as he looked: he had a van on the other side of the street. An accomplice was at the wheel and the engine was running. Seconds later the van was roaring off.

'Just leave my notes!' screamed Georgie.

The brutish-looking individual, having belied his appearance in the stupidity stakes, now did so in the kindness department as well. He threw Georgie's bag out of the speeding van.

Almost sobbing with relief, Georgie ran to retrieve it and the scattered notes from the street.

Jez, meanwhile, had extracted a mini-telescope (as you do) from his trouser pocket and was calmly reciting the number plate of the van to himself. 'A TO5 OF,' he repeated. 'Shouldn't be difficult to remember.'

'Scumbag,' said Dylan. 'Doesn't it make you sick when people rip you off like that?' Then, scratching his head in disbelief, he ambled over to Georgie to help her retrieve her notes.

'I don't believe this,' moaned Georgie, scrabbling about in the wet gutter.

'God,' said Dylan, looking at the smudged papers. 'They've ruined all your typing.' Feeling genuinely sorry for her, he squatted down beside her.

'And,' she sniffed as she searched her handbag, 'they've taken my keys.'

'Hey, don't worry.' Dylan patted her arm. 'We'll sort out the notes and we'll get your keys back. Meanwhile,' he added with a smile, 'why don't you come home and have a nice cup of tea with us?'

'I didn't think Americans had nice cups of tea.'

Dylan frowned. Was she being rude or funny? Funny, he decided. He was the one who wanted to get rude. 'Well,' he said with a shrug, 'I've lived here for five years. I'm learning – *trying* – to get civilized.'

Despite her annoyance over the scam, the money, the notes and, indeed, the entire day, Georgie was tempted. She was dying to know what sort of place these two lived in. And *normal* wasn't the word suggesting itself at the back of her mind.

The Gasometer

Here we are, then. At the gasometer. At last. Gasometers are not, in the general scheme of things, normal places to live. They are those huge cylindrical structures dotted around depressing parts of cities. Think massive tin drum. This was where Dylan and Jez met. And this was now their home.

Georgie, of course, had no idea that she was about to have her nice cup of tea in the urban equivalent of a grain silo. When Jez pulled up in a depressing street in a depressing part of London, she felt vaguely depressed and not a little disappointed. Where was the wacky apartment she had anticipated? Where the post-modernist, deconstructionist, minimalist ergonomic loft? Surely not in one of these gloomy, uniform semis that lined the street? A snob Georgie was not – although she could, with some justification, have been one (more of which later) – but she had been so sure that Jez and Dylan would live somewhere that reflected their eccentricity. And here she was smack in the bosom of net-curtain land.

'Here we are,' said Dylan, opening his door and leaping out in front of a particularly grim little number.

Georgie was appalled. This house and its immediate neighbours were even worse than the others in the street. There was some sort of huge, ghastly industrial structure looming behind it, plunging it into a hellish gloom. It, and Georgie.

'I didn't,' she said bleakly, 'imagine you living in a place like this.'

'No,' said Jez as, forgetting there was no rear window, he pointlessly locked the car. 'Not many people do.'

But Georgie wasn't listening. She was looking at Dylan. He was heading, not for the front door of the house, but for a little gate between it and its neighbour. On the gate was a placard reading THAMES GAS. PRIVATE PROPERTY. KEEP OUT.

Dylan went through the gate, gesturing for Georgie to follow. Shrugging, Georgie obeyed. Jez brought up the rear. When he reached the gate he opened a large box beside it and, to Georgie's astonishment, emptied the voluminous amounts of mail it contained into the large bag he was carrying. Then, grinning, he followed Georgie through the gate.

The pathway on the other side led past the houses and directly towards a small door in the towering gasometer.

A slow smile began to play at the corners of Georgie's mouth. They didn't, she told herself. They couldn't possibly.

But they could. And they did.

The little door gave onto a short walkway inside the structure and then onto the vast, cathedral-like expanse of the interior.

Georgie could hardly believe her eyes. What could have been vulgar and tasteless was instead a harmonious blend of old and new, of classic and modern. The Georgian pillars flanking the entrance were, in turn, flanked by two statues of Greek gods – wearing motorcycle helmets. The huge bookcase in one corner stood next to a life-size model of Batman; the paintings were alternately copies of old masters and post-modernist abstracts. Here, there was a wall of exquisite Georgian panelling; there, a fifties-style seating area. There were Persian rugs, strangely beautiful light sculptures, an electric-blue kitchen area, juke boxes and, on either side of the open-plan space, two greenhouses. One wall, Georgie noticed in amusement, was entirely papered with a collage of pictures of stately homes. And beside it, on a battered table, stood a cardboard model of another.

'I –' stammered Georgie.

'Sorry about the mess,' interrupted Jez. 'We've had trouble getting a cleaner.' Then he tipped the contents of his bag onto the floor and turned back to her. 'Tea or coffee?'

Still reeling, Georgie found herself incapable of speech.

A concerned Jez thought it was because of the mess. He bent down to a leopardskin sofa and plumped up a cushion. 'There,' he said, 'that's better.' What else, he wondered, did nice middle-class people do? Ah. The nice cup of tea. He threaded his way past a large plastic killer whale suspended from the ceiling and popped on the kettle.

'Tea or coffee?' he prompted again.

'Er . . . coffee, thanks.'

Jez frowned. 'Sorry about the smell,' he said with a grimace. 'It's –'

'Gas?' Georgie, he was delighted to see, was grinning.

'Yes!' Then, with another frown, 'How did you guess?'

Georgie shrugged. 'Oh, you know . . . intuition.' Then

she stepped forward to the pile of mail on the floor. 'You get a lot of catalogues and magazines,' she mused.

'Yes.' Jez was busying himself with the tea things. 'Competitions.'

'Competitions?'

'Yes. We do a lot of competitions. Y'know . . . tie-breaks . . . complete-in-not-more-than-seven-words . . . that sort of thing.'

'Why?'

Jez, puzzled, looked across at her. 'In order to win.'

'Oh.' That, Georgie supposed, seemed reasonable enough. 'What have you won so far?'

'Practically everything.'

'But what do you do with it?'

'Well, some of it we sell,' said Jez, pointing to five hundred kitsch china dolls in the corner. 'Others we keep. But only,' he finished, 'if they're really useful.' As he spoke, he patted an industrial-sized soda fountain.

'Ah. I see. Mind if I look around?'

Jez professed himself to be delighted. Dylan was busy on the telephone, an activity that had consumed him from the moment he had returned home. Georgie edged her way past a free-standing wall papered with pictures of stately homes, past a rather beautiful if slightly battered cardboard model of another one and towards one of the greenhouses.

'Bedroom,' said Jez.

'Ah. Silly me.' Indeed it was a bedroom, and, judging by the rail of expensive suits, it was Dylan's. Feeling suddenly guilty, Georgie headed to its opposite number. It contained few clothes, was catastrophically untidy and strewn with computer magazines. Jez's.

Behind her, coffee made, Jez decided that the next,

normal thing to do was to play some music. Make Georgie feel welcome. He headed towards the massive jukebox in the corner and selected a Burt Bacharach record. As Burt began to croon, a bank of dancing plants startled the life out of Georgie as they kicked into action.

'Non-dairy creamer?' asked Jez, now back in the kitchen.

'I beg your pardon?'

Jez held up a small carton – one of three thousand – and showed it to Georgie. 'No cows. Stays fresh.'

'Uh . . . black, please.' Georgie stepped forward, accepted the proffered mug and sat down at the bar counter. 'Tasty,' she said, as she took a sip.

'Um . . .' Jez looked suddenly uncomfortable. 'Yes.'

They lapsed into silence. Dylan, however, made up for their quietness. 'Is that the DVLC?' they heard him say. 'Yes . . . I'm expecting the registration documents for my van. Yes,' he repeated after a moment, 'it's A TO5 OF.'

Georgie raised an eyebrow at Jez. 'The getaway van?'

Jez nodded.

'I'm terribly sorry,' purred Dylan down the line, 'but could you tell me if you've sent it to my new or old address?' As he spoke, he turned to Jez and made a *pen and paper* gesture. Jez leaped to his feet and grabbed both from the box beside the gigantic fridge. '154 Stanley Grove,' said Dylan after a moment. 'No, that's fine. Thank you.'

Dylan replaced the receiver, winked at Jez and Georgie, and then picked it up again. This time, when his call was eventually answered, Dylan adopted an entirely different tone.

'Yes,' he screamed, 'you *can* help me. I booked four tickets for Andrew Lloyd Webber's musical last night.

When I turned up, the seats had gone and there was no record of our booking. As a result,' he continued after a pause for more angry breath, 'we had to stand in the rain for forty-five minutes and my youngest, Jessica, caught a throat infection. She is now,' he said with tearful anguish, 'lying in bed, her glands are dangerously high and . . . and the girl's a goddam asthmatic! Now what,' he screamed hysterically, 'are you going to do about it?'

Then Dylan covered the mouthpiece with his hand and smiled over at the others. 'Jez,' he said in a calm, friendly voice, 'why don't you show her the Van der Graph thingy?'

'Good idea.' Jez stood up. 'You want it see it?'

'Er . . . yes.'

'*What?*' shouted Dylan down the phone. 'What? Four complimentary tickets? Yeah. Sure. Two in the stalls, two in the circle . . . . yes, my wife's afraid of heights. Yes . . . and my son's long-sighted. For the night after tomorrow. Sure – it's Ricky Lee Hasselhöff. Umlaut on the "o".' Breathing deeply and smiling broadly, Dylan replaced the phone once again.

Before he made his next call, he picked up the extension lead of the instrument and fiddled around at the join of the two cords. Then, with the join in one hand, he picked up the handset with the other.

'Operator?' Irritation rather than extreme anger was evidently the theme of this call. 'I've rung before: this is 0181 3613 2546. Right? Right. Well, I'm sorry,' he said as he fiddled again with the join in the cords, 'but the crackle is still on the line . . . you can hear it? Good. Well, I would like a refund on the last fifty calls I've made and a reduction in my rental charge for the next month. What? Yes, of course I'll write . . . is it freepost?'

Freepost it was, and, with a sigh of satisfaction, Dylan replaced the handset for the last time that day.

Over by a workbench (second prize in a DIY tie-break), Jez was demonstrating the Van der Graph generator. 'It's a static electricity machine. Y'see, if I crank this handle it'll start spitting –'

'Oh my God! There's blue lightning going up your finger and –'

'And my hair's standing on end?' Jez started to laugh. 'It's all right . . . can you pass me one of those strip lights?'

This, thought Georgie, is totally bizarre. But rather fun, she had to admit. She felt as if she was Alice in Wonderland trespassing in Aladdin's cave. She handed a fluorescent tube to Jez. As he touched it, the tube lit up and so, because she was still holding the other end, did Georgie's face. She could feel her hair beginning to stand on end.

Jez, equally delighted, laughed at her. 'That's how these lights work, you see. Off static electricity. The static acti-vates particles in the tube, causing molecular friction, and it lights up.'

Jez, thought Georgie, is a different person when he's in his element. What had happened to the tongue-tied anorak of earlier today?

He had disappeared. Grinning like a schoolboy, Jez took his hand off the tube, leaving it with Georgie. It went out. Then, shyly, he reached for her other hand. A frisson of electricity (Lana and Clark would have enjoyed this game) shot between them and the tube lit up again.

'That,' laughed Georgie, 'is wonderful. Wonderful.'

Then Dylan, also laughing, delighting both in their game and in the results of his telephone calls, came over to join them. Putting his arms round their shoulders and his face between theirs, he hugged them both to him.

'Just one more little job,' he said.

The light went out.

Dylan frowned and grabbed Jez's and Georgie's hands. 'Hey!' he laughed as the light flickered on again. 'Neat!'

Georgie giggled again, and then, as Dylan bent closer to her, stopped abruptly. Gosh, she thought, he's handsome.

Jez was thinking much the same thing (and no there's no funny business looming. After all, this is a *family* saga. Jez was simply jealous.)

'Georgie,' said Dylan, 'will you do me the pleasure of coming to the theatre with me in two days' time?'

Georgie giggled again in an attempt to hide her surprise. After a moment she said, 'Do you always take your secretarial staff out to the theatre after their first day?'

'Well . . .' Dylan looked smug, 'it is a bit of a tradition, yes.'

'Well . . . . who am I to deprive an American of what little tradition he can get? Yes – I'd be delighted to come.'

Unseen by the other two, the light went out of Jez's eyes.

Georgie's House

Both of them were itching to see where Georgie lived. Dylan because he was perennially nosy and Jez because . . . well, because it was where Georgie lived. They had driven her home, escorted her out of the car, and were now standing with her outside the stained-glass front door of the Edwardian house in Chelsea. But Georgie was having none of it.

'So,' she said, ringing the bell. 'Thank you both.' Then, to Dylan, 'And about the rest of my money . . . ?' Dylan still owed her seventy-five pounds.

Dylan tapped a fist against his heart. Or possibly his wallet. 'I'll have it at the theatre,' he replied with a reassuring smile.

'You'd better. Or else it'll be curtains.'

'Curtains up – or curtains down?' joked Dylan.

But whoever else lived in Georgie's house had answered the bell. Turning to the entryphone, Georgie shouted, 'It's only me! I've . . . er, lost my keys.'

Dylan and Jez exchanged curious glances.

Then the door sprang open, Georgie slipped inside and banged it shut behind her.

'Some gal,' said Dylan, after a surprised pause.

'Yes,' sulked Jez as they turned back to the car. 'Some girl you're flirting with.'

Dylan raised an eyebrow. 'Hey! You've fallen!'

'No, I have not.'

Dylan poked him in the ribs. 'You fancy her. But,' he added, 'you're wasting your time.'

'I know, I know. You're good-looking and I'm too technical.' This, evidently, was not the first time they had trodden this particular conversational route.

'Jez! Stop punishing yourself . . . you're not too technical. You're just ugly.'

'I am,' said Jez, not remotely offended by the remark, 'but I can't help it.' Then, looking suddenly sad, he shook his head. 'I can see them start to drift off,' he said in a small voice. 'It's like they're begging me to stop. I try and be like I am with you but –'

Dylan silenced him with a heartfelt squeeze on the shoulder. He hated it when Jez got like this. 'You're just nervous,' he consoled. 'You should relax. At the moment, you see, you're totally shag-proof.'

'Thanks, Dylan.'

'Well . . . I'm not saying you should take a leaf out of my book . . .'

'But?'

'But you should.'

They both laughed. An eavesdropper on their conversation might have suggested that Dylan needed a good smack round the head. But Jez would have been appalled by the suggestion. His friend, he knew, would go to the ends of the earth for him – even if the journey meant a detour past as many pretty girls as he could find. Dylan just couldn't help himself.

Dylan, on the other hand, wished that Jez *could* help himself. To as many pretty girls as he could find.

'What,' asked Jez, breaking the pensive silence as they climbed back into the car, 'was that last little job you were talking about?'

'Our friend who stole the laptop and Georgie's keys.'

'Oh, yeah. I'd forgotten.'

'I've got a little surprise for him.'

'Good. I like surprises.'

'He's not going to like this one.'

'No,' said Jez as he gunned the engine. 'I can't imagine he will.'

Dave Ray is the brutish-looking individual who rams crow-bars through the rear windows of Rovers but who has, it must not be forgotten, some redeeming features.

His taste in interior decoration is not one of them – although the riot of vulgarity that is number 154, Stanley Grove could be attributable to his wife. Yet she, on the evening that Dylan and Jez were to pay their clandestine visit, was not available for discussions about offensive soft furnishings. She was, in fact, curled up on one of the offenders – an apricot velour sofa – watching taped reruns of her favourite Brazilian soap opera. Dave was also in the room, trying to fathom the mysterious depths of Jez's laptop. He wasn't getting very far and would probably have been happier with a black box, a speaker, a microphone and a brick. Nevertheless, he tapped away at every key he could find, punctuating his efforts with an impressive variety of salty swearwords. Solace for his frustration was further provided from the contents of a large and greasy carton of something that purported to be fried chicken and chips. Babs contented herself with Twiglets.

It was just another normal evening *chez* Ray.

Except that it wasn't. Outside and half a block away, a battered Rover 90 had just drawn to a halt, disgorging Dylan from one side and Jez from the other. A short, heated conversation took place, after which both men ran with exaggerated stealth to number 154, Stanley Grove.

Reaching it, they crouched beneath the window of Babs's lounge (see? It was her after all) and then, after another, shorter but even more heated conversation, raised their heads simultaneously for a quick peek into the room. They were at once gratified and appalled by what they saw. Gratified, because the Rays were at home; appalled, because they both felt immediately sorry for anyone obliged to spend an entire evening surrounded by flock wallpaper, swirly carpets, a day-glo fishtank and enough assorted knick-knacks to keep a bingo hall in fat ladies for several years. 'It takes a great deal of money,' whispered Dylan, 'to make a place look this cheap.' Then he winced when he saw Babs – a recent convert from smoking – stub out a Twiglet in the sombrero compartment of an ashtray marked TORREMOLINOS. Jez winced when he saw Dave stabbing at his keyboard with stubby, chickeny fingers. Then they lowered their heads and, exchanging an understanding look rather than a heated exchange, scurried away.

Inside the house, Babs groaned as the Brazilian soap reached its climax with the death of the hero, the suicide of the heroine, the torching of the family's *hacienda* and the general agreement of the show's producers that the soap had been a non-starter in the first place.

Babs channel-hopped for a few minutes and then, cursing the lack of anything watchable, picked up the latest issue of *Hi!*. Contentedly burying herself in the minutiae of the charming drawing room of the lesser branch of Albania's royal family, she was totally oblivious to the activity on the TV screen.

So was Dave.

And so were Jez and Dylan. They were too busy hot-wiring Dave's van.

All in all, the situation was highly ironic. Pleasingly so for two of those involved – not so for the other two. For

Babs's television was broadcasting the information that, in the last year, car theft had increased in London by twenty per cent.

4

Dylan and Jez had different, and arguably more construc-
tive, ways to relax than did most people. After a full day's
work at InfoTec, an interesting interlude with Georgie and
then spot of van-stealing, they were ready to chill out at
the gasometer.

Here is an example of their methods:

Dylan: '"You'll be shocked by what's to try on . . . when
you shop at the World of Nylon". Is that good?'

Jez: 'Beautiful – but how about this one: "In not
more than eight words, explain why you buy Zappy
Nappies".'

Dylan (a sigh, followed by the consumption of one of

the free biscuits they had won in a recent competition): 'I don't know . . . that's a tough one.' Then, counting on his fingers, '"I buy Zappy Nappies for my kid's . . ." Shit, I've run out of words.'

Jez (with a grin): 'We could just try that.'

'What? "I buy Zappy Nappies for my kid's shit"?' Dylan was appalled.

'Well,' said Jez, chewing his pencil, 'at least it's honest.'

Dylan looked over to his friend. 'Where,' he said with a teasing grin, 'did honesty ever get you?'

Jez pondered that one. He had, he told himself, been law-abiding for most of his young life. He had interviewed for job after job. He had failed, time after time, to secure job after job. And then he had landed job after unfulfilling job. And then he had met Dylan and his life had changed forever.

'Well,' he said, 'honesty will get me one year's supply of Zappy Nappies.'

'Is there something you haven't told me? Are you heavy with child?'

Jez grinned over towards where Dylan, now dressed in a sweatshirt and jogging pants, was hauling himself up and down on an exercise bar (third prize in a fitness-literacy competition). 'Yeah,' he said absently.

'Congratulations!' yelled Dylan. 'So what do you want with a year's supply of nappies?' Despite sounding dismissive, Dylan was genuinely interested. This, after all, was how they made their living when they weren't engaged in high-profile jobs like the InfoTec scam.

Jez continued to chew his pencil. 'In one of those baby-care CD ROMs,' he explained, 'it says that a baby relieves himself eight point two times a day.'

'Hmm . . .' Dylan stopped hauling. 'Eight point two.'

'Yes. Therefore, he gets his nappy changed once every three hours – to avoid chapping.'

'Isn't that a little rash?'

Jez ignored him. 'Which is two thousand nine hundred and twenty nappies a year.'

Dylan left the bar and came over to sit beside Jez. 'So . . . if a pack of fifty costs about eight bucks –'

'Pounds.'

'– pounds. That makes . . .'

'Four hundred and sixty-seven pounds and twenty pence a year. So,' finished Jez, putting down the pencil, 'we sell them half price to Gary, who'll collect, and we make about two hundred and thirty-three quid.'

Jez was nothing if not mathematically competent.

And Dylan, though dyslexic, could muster a damn fine jingle. '"Zappy Nappies",' he declared with triumph, '"Make Baby Happy!"'

A week later they won a year's supply of nappies.

The next morning dawned bright and clear and sunny – although not in the gasometer. The disadvantage of the building – apart from the rather obvious fact that it wasn't a stately home – was that it had no windows.

Dylan, too, was bright and clear and sunny in the morning. He demonstrated this by bounding into Jez's greenhouse, leaping on his bed and pummelling him into wakefulness.

'Up!' he barked.

'Nnngh,' replied Jez.

'No, really. We've got to go.'

Jez opened one eye. 'Where?'

Dylan jumped off the bed. He was, Jez noted blearily, wearing a baggy white jumpsuit.

'Why are you wearing a baggy white jumpsuit?'

'Because,' grinned Dylan, throwing a similar item at Jez's head, 'I'd hate to clash with you.'

The plot, as they say, was thickening.

Ten minutes later they left the gasometer and leaped, courtesy of the unwitting Dave Ray, into the white van. 'Where are we going?' mumbled Jez.

'Nowhere – unless you hot-wire this thing again. It's so selfish,' added Dylan, sounding genuinely cross, 'of people not to leave their keys in their vehicles.'

'Yeah,' said Jez, from underneath the steering block. 'Downright inconsiderate.'

Then, as the engine sparked into life, someone banged on the side of the van. Jez and Dylan exchanged a fearful look. Not, surely, the police? Not, heaven forbid, the brutish-looking owner with the appalling taste in interior design? Not already. It was far too early for the van to have been reported stolen.

But, to their intense surprise, their visitor was none other than Georgie.

'Georgie!' Then they peered more closely at her. She looked dreadful. 'Georgie?'

'My bag,' she replied, rubbing the other, even heavier, bags under her eyes. 'The notes. I left them in your car.'

'You look tired,' said Dylan. Jez remained silent. While thrilled to see Georgie, he was desperately concerned about her appearance.

'I'm exhausted. I didn't get any sleep at all last night.'

So what, thought both men, was she doing instead?

The Devil

Georgie was in a nightclub. Her spiky hair was swept back
into a sleek, shiny bob; her make-up was vampily dramatic
– all pouting red lips and dark, come-hither eyes. Her
indecently short little black dress left absolutely nothing to
the imagination. She was reclining on a piano, surrounded
by ogling men. In one gloved hand she held a champagne
flute and in the other an elegant cigarette holder. She
reclined further and crossed her legs, displaying even more
thigh and her impossibly high stilettos. And then she put
her cigarette to her lips and, slowly and invitingly, puffed
a column of smoke into Dylan's face.

The Angel

Georgie was sitting at a scrubbed wooden table in a sparsely
furnished garret. The only light came from a single flickering
candle; the only warmth from the sad embers in the fireplace.
But Georgie didn't care; her own discomfort meant nothing
to her. Her attention was entirely focused on the tiny baby
squirrel in front of her. Wrapped in her grey cardigan, the
little creature at last seemed to be winning its battle for life.
Now accepting the drops of milk Georgie was feeding him,
he was staring at her through dark, soulful eyes, silently
thanking her for saving him. For the first time since her long
vigil began, Georgie smiled. Not to herself – self-indulgence
was for others – but to her companions in the room. The
rabbits and the deer, tenderly watching the baby squirrel,
smiled back. Above them, the doves cooed softly.

*   *   *

Georgie was beginning to get annoyed. Jez and Dylan had retreated into a dopey silence: Dylan wearing a lascivious smile, Jez a beatific calm one. 'I said,' she repeated, 'that I left my bag in your car.'

'Oh.' Jez became suddenly animated. 'Sorry, Georgie.' He sprang out of the van and ran to the nearby Rover.

Dylan, too, came back to life. 'Hey,' he said. 'Yesterday, with the paper bag . . . How d'you know about that? You . . . uh, you hit first aid in high school, or what?'

'No. Medical school.'

Dylan looked impressed. 'Ah . . . I see. The notes.' He threw her an apologetic smile. 'Sorry, I get it now. You're a typist at medical school.'

'I'm training,' snapped Georgie, 'to be a doctor.'

'Wow! A doctor, huh?' Dylan nodded to himself. 'A doctor with secretarial skills. Wow.'

Georgie couldn't help grinning. Dylan wasn't being patronizing. He was just being Dylan.

Jez returned, panting, with Georgie's bag of notes. 'Here,' he said, handing them over with a puppy-like grin.

'Thanks.' Clearly not in the mood for small talk, Georgie moved away. Then, remembering, she turned back. 'Oh, Jez, I meant to ask you yesterday. What's the name of the orphanage you donate to?'

Jez froze. 'It's . . . er . . . um . . . it's . . .'

'It's a very personal matter,' said Dylan, adopting a holier-than-thou expression. 'We give, but we don't like to talk about it. We're very like Phil Collins in that respect.'

'I can see then,' replied Georgie, 'why you don't like to talk about it.'

Dylan neatly changed the subject. 'What,' he asked, 'are you doing today?'

'I have to study.'

'Won't you allow us the pleasure of feeding you breakfast first?'

Georgie wavered for a moment. Then, realizing she was starving as well as exhausted, she nodded and accompanied Jez into the van.

Dylan was driving. This, he realized too late, was a disadvantage in the Georgie-seducing department. But not as far as Jez was concerned. Sitting in between them in the front seat, she lasted all of one minute before she fell asleep on Jez's shoulder.

Noting Dylan's expression, Jez went on the defensive. 'All it means is that she's relaxed in our company.'

'If she relaxes any more,' replied Dylan, noting Georgie's open mouth and the little dribble of saliva trickling down her chin, 'it could get very messy.'

'Don't. She might hear.'

'Nah. She won't. She's wrecked. God knows,' he added with a wicked grin, 'what she was up to last night.'

'I don't care,' sniffed Jez, wondering whether or not to drape his right arm over Georgie's shoulders. It would certainly be happier there than in its current, embarrassed position by the roof. But he didn't dare. Instead, he looked down at the sleeping girl. 'No,' he repeated. 'I don't care. She's got charm and warmth and –'

'And neat little sit-up breasts.'

Jez sighed in exasperation. Then he remembered that Dylan couldn't help lowering the tone. He was, after all, American.

They drove in companionable silence for another ten minutes before Jez remembered he didn't know where they were going – or why.

'Where're we going, Dylan? You still haven't told me.'

'Holland Park.'

'Nice. Why?'

'To lay loft insulation.'

'Loft insulation?'

'Yes.'

Jez looked down at his Michelin-man outfit. 'So this is what loft insulators wear?'

'Seems appropriate. They were, after all, fourth prize in that "Warmth for Winter" competition.'

'I think that was about insulating yourself, not your loft.'

'I know, but then we got third prize in that DIY competition and that's where I got the idea.'

'What idea?'

Dylan reached into his pocket and handed Jez an identity badge. It was not dissimilar to yesterday's VerbaTec badge. It was, in fact, the same badge with a different name on the paper insert.

'LofTec,' said Jez, reading the card. 'I like it. So what was the third prize in the DIY? I don't remember.'

Dylan sighed. Sometimes Jez could be remarkably dense. 'Loft insulating material.'

'Oh, right. And we pick it up in Holland Park?'

'No.' Dylan took one hand off the wheel, reached behind him and pulled the sliding door to the rear of the van. 'It's here.'

Careful not to disturb the slumbering Georgie, Jez craned his neck to view the contents of the van: several rolls of yellow insulating fibre.

'What I don't understand,' he said after a moment's thought, 'is how the man who stole my laptop also managed to get his hands on our insulating rolls.'

'He didn't. I put them there this morning.'

'Ah. Dylan?'

'Mmm?'

'When do I get my laptop back?'

'Tomorrow night.'

'Good.' Jez grinned. 'Ah . . . of course. That's what the theatre's all about.'

'You got it.'

Again a happy silence reigned in the van. A happy silence of mutual understanding. It was probably just as well Georgie was asleep. She, poor thing, would have been utterly confused by their conversation. As would anyone else.

Ten minutes later Dylan drew to a halt in a road that, like many roads in Holland Park, screamed money. Old money, mainly. But there was, to the chagrin of Mrs Stratton-Luce at number one, Cranworth Crescent, a clutch of nouveaux at the other end. On the other hand, a Tracey or two did give one something to talk about at dinner parties.

Dylan knew the names of everyone on Cranworth Crescent. He even knew Mrs Stratton-Luce's darkest and most shameful secret: her middle name was Sharon. Mrs Stratton-Luce was under the impression that she had consigned that name to history, that after years of diligent obliteration there no evidence to link her with those disgusting syllables. She was wrong. The electoral roll knew all about Eleanor Bridget Felicity Sharon Stratton-Luce. And so did Dylan.

After parking the van, Dylan reached into the glove compartment and pulled out a blueprint of Cranworth Crescent (courtesy of the land registry) and a list (from the electoral roll) of its inhabitants. Then, remembering his invitation to Georgie, he extracted a parcel containing several rashers of bacon wrapped in foil and a loaf of bread. 'First things first,' he said, opening his door. Then he walked round to the front of the van, opened the bonnet and placed the bacon on the radiator.

Several minutes later he had constructed three perfectly cooked bacon sandwiches. Careful not to arouse the comatose Georgie, Jez wriggled away from her and exited the van just in time to stop Dylan stealing the third sandwich. 'She might want it when she wakes up,' Jez protested, grabbing his own and leaning through the open window to deposit Georgie's on the dashboard.

'Giving women the vote,' mused Dylan, 'was a massive constitutional mistake.'

'What'll we do with her?'

Dylan shrugged. 'She looks happy enough there. We won't be long anyway. Let's just leave her.'

How nice, thought Jez, to have Georgie to come back to.

A moment later, leaving the sleeping Georgie and the congealing bacon roll in the van, they walked into the clinically neat garden of number one and, carrying their rolls of insulation under their arms, marched up the path to the front door.

Eleanor Stratton-Luce answered the bell, as she did most things, with intimidating alacrity. And she looked, as indeed she usually looked, with extreme distaste at the two men on her doorstep.

'Yes?' she drawled. 'Can I help you?' Her tone implied that she rather doubted it.

'Mrs Stratton-Luce?' enquired Dylan in an accent that startled the life out of Jez. For some reason, Dylan had decided that loft insulators should not only dress like

Michelin men but should speak in a clipped Home Counties accent. Or rather, a shockingly bad imitation of a Home Counties accent.

Mrs Stratton-Luce bristled with indignation at the mispronunciation of her hallowed name. 'Yes,' she snapped, glaring at the strange apparitions in the white jump suits. 'What do you want?'

Dylan offered her his dazzling smile and, for a fleeting and wicked moment, wondered if he should inform her that he was aware of her shameful secret. Would her accent slip in horror, her Alice band fall off in shock, her pleated skirt rumple in dismay? The edifice that was Eleanor would crumble before him.

But Dylan didn't want Eleanor to crumble. He wanted her to give him money. 'James,' he said, 'asked us to come round to slot in some insulation for your new abode.'

'Oh.' Mrs Stratton-Luce took a step back into a hallway that looked as if it were wearing a uniform. Neat, tidy, correct and unexcitingly inoffensive, it was, Dylan suspected, identical to every other hallway in the street. Mrs Stratton-Luce, always alert to the threat of contagious diseases, retreated even further. 'I suppose you'd better come in.'

Dylan stepped forward. 'Did James,' he said, almost casually, 'leave you the fifty pounds cash?'

The Alice band quivered. 'No. He did not.' James's greatest fault – and it had a great many to compete with – was his terminal meanness.

'Well . . .' Dylan pondered the problem for a moment. 'If you could scrape it together,' he said with an endearing grin, 'we could have the job done in a few minutes and you won't lose your fifty pounds deposit.'

That clinched it as far as Mrs Stratton-Luce was concerned. Losing deposits smacked of inefficiency. Worse, it was horribly common. 'Oh. Well, in that case . . .'

'Thwartman,' said Dylan to Jez, 'if you could start getting the hardware in . . .'

Jez shot Dylan a particularly vicious look. *Thwartman?* And only fifty pounds? What on earth was Dylan thinking of? They could have made far more money by flogging the stuff.

Jez had to wait until they were out of Mrs Stratton-Luce's earshot before voicing his doubts. And as he suspected – correctly – that Mrs Stratton-Luce had perfect hearing, this meant he had to wait until they were alone in the attic.

'Why on earth,' he said as Dylan began to unroll the insulation, 'are we insulating this woman's loft for fifty pounds?'

'Trust me. Wait and see.' Dylan began to lay the material between the joists of the floor. 'And you could, while you're at it, help me.'

Jez sighed and bent down. 'I just can't believe we're doing this. We earned a small fortune yesterday. I mean . . . fifty pounds? Even if we do another house –'

'We are.'

'– we'll make less money that we could have got from selling the stuff.'

'Is there a problem?' To their horror, the Alice band appeared at the trapdoor. Beneath it appeared Mrs Stratton-Luce and her haughtily disdainful features.

'No,' said Dylan. 'We're very nearly finished.'

Mrs Stratton-Luce looked around. Tradesmen, in her opinion, were not to be trusted. One never knew, did one? Give them an inch, and they would undoubtedly take a mile. Let them use the lavatory and next minute they'd be robbing the safe. And of course, one had learned one's lesson about tea – one had simply stopped offering it. Three sugars indeed. Completely excessive and, ultimately, ruinously expensive. Did they think one was made of money?

Still, Mrs Stratton-Luce found herself grudgingly admitting that these two looked respectable enough. And they were quick workers – even if they did chatter non-stop in their funny little accents. 'Well,' she said, still peering above the trapdoor, 'you won't leave any mess, will you?'

'No, Mrs Stratton-Luce. You won't even know we've been here,' said Dylan. This, did Mrs Stratton-Luce but know it, was a piercingly accurate remark. But she didn't know it, so descended from the attic and readdressed herself, in her pristine drawing room, to the seating plan for tonight's dinner party. One had to get these things absolutely spot on.

Five minutes later, she heard the tradesmen on the stairs and shot into the hallway, closing the door firmly behind her. 'Finished?' she asked, scouring the carpet for dirty footprints.

'All done, Mrs Stratton-Luce,' replied Dylan with his dazzling smile.

'Hmm.' Mrs Stratton-Luce was beginning to feel rather out of sorts. There was no such thing, in her experience, as a perfect workman. They must have done *something* wrong.

But they hadn't. The attic, when Dylan escorted her back up, was perfect. There was no mess. There were no dirty footprints on the stair carpet and no cigarette stubs in the aspidistra. It was all frightfully disappointing.

'Well,' she said as she ushered them to the front door. 'James will be pleased.'

No, he won't, thought Dylan. 'Er . . .'

'Oh, yes.' Mrs Stratton-Luce unclenched her palm. 'Fifty, was it?'

'It was.' Dylan took the proffered notes and, with a final smile, tapped his forehead in, Mrs Stratton-Luce was glad to see, a gesture of deference. 'Regards to James,' he added.

Mrs Stratton-Luce thought that rather cheeky.

Back at the van, Georgie was still sound asleep. Beside her, the bacon roll was looking baleful. Dylan opened the rear of the van and hauled out the remaining roll of insulation.

'I am not,' repeated Jez, 'doing another one.'

'Yes, you are.'

'We don't have enough.'

Dylan threw the roll at him. 'I know, but that's irrelevant. Trustingness,' he added as he headed towards number three, 'is next to godliness.'

Mrs Gosling was certainly trusting. 'How silly of Charles not to tell me,' she said as she escorted them through a hallway identical to the one next door. 'And to think how long I've been badgering him about getting insulation.'

'Maybe,' ventured Dylan, 'he thought it would be a nice surprise.'

'Yes.' What a nice young man, thought Mrs Gosling. 'He probably did. He likes surprises.'

Not this one, thought Dylan, as he climbed into the loft.

'Dylan?' Jez followed him up the ladder and looked around. 'Dylan?' Where on earth, he thought, scratching his head, can he have got to? The loft wasn't exactly spacious: it was identical to the one next door.

'Je-ez.' Well, there was the voice – but where was the man?

He was next door.

The plans purloined from the land registry had been detailed and highly accurate in their specifications. They had informed Dylan that all the houses in Cranworth Crescent had interconnecting attics. Few of the residents themselves knew that – most of them would have been horrified by the very idea. Yet it was a fact: at the top of the eaves in every attic was a small space, a sort of duct that led to the house next door. Dylan had disappeared through the duct.

'Dylan? You next door?'

'Yep. Just a minute.' On the other side, Jez could hear sounds of folding and rolling. The next minute, one of the rolls of insulation so charmingly installed in Mrs Stratton-Luce's attic hurtled through the hole in the wall. It was followed by Dylan, grinning from ear to ear. 'See?'

'You mean . . .' Jez looked to where Dylan was pointing, to the opposite side of the attic, to the wall shared with number five. Then he walked over, hoisted himself up and looked through the gap in the eaves. It gave onto the next house where, in turn, there was a gap leading to the next house and –

'There are thirty-five houses on this side of the street,' said Dylan. 'That's thirty-five times fifty pounds.'

Jez turned to face him. Like Dylan, he was giggling. 'Sometimes,' he said, 'you really do amaze me.'

'I know,' said Dylan, vaulting over to number one to deprive Mrs Stratton-Luce of her last roll of insulation. 'I often amaze myself.'

Practice, thought Jez, makes perfect. By the time they had reached number twenty-nine, they could insulate an attic in ten minutes. And de-insulate it as well. A few houses down the line, they changed their technique and, after showing the proud lady of the house her new insulation, they ripped it up again and hurled it over to the next house. Then they went downstairs to collect their fifty pounds.

Mrs Carter-Ross was highly impressed by their efficiency. Mrs Green was delighted by their speed. And Mrs Wentworth was utterly charmed by how polite they were. The only householder to remain unmoved by their work was Tracey Slattery at number twenty-seven. She, as she made it abundantly clear to Dylan, had ideas about laying that had nothing to do with insulation. Dylan declined – but politely.

They didn't encounter a single problem until they reached number thirty-three. Mrs Cummins was appalled that Robert would have contemplated insulation without informing her.

'I wonder,' she said with a worried frown, 'where he got the money for that?' The frown deepened. 'How much is it?'

'It's only fifty pounds.'

Mrs Cummins was shocked. She looked wide-eyed at Dylan. 'Fifty pounds? I know Rob thought we needed insulation, but I'm surprised he felt we could afford it what with all the new bills for pooper-scooper bins and so on.' Then, with a weary sigh, she gestured for them to come in. 'Oh well, maybe I could find the money from the savings tin.'

Dylan and Jez exchanged a quick look. This, the look

said, wasn't on. Robin Hood wouldn't have touched this with a bargepole. 'Mrs Cummins,' suggested Jez, 'why don't we come back another day?'

'Yes,' agreed Dylan. 'We might even be doing a special in a few weeks' time.'

Mrs Cummins's relief was palpable. 'Thank you, love,' she sighed, 'I think that would be better.'

'I have,' said Dylan as they made their way next door, 'an idea.'

'Yes,' said Jez. 'So do I.'

'One that would appeal to Robin?'

Jez smiled and nodded.

Next door, Mrs Furnival-Jones posed a problem of a different sort. While she merely *tutted* about Richard forgetting to leave fifty pounds, she was a stickler for perfection. Twice she poked her head through the trapdoor, searching, Stratton-Luce-like, for imperfection. Then, when invited to inspect the finished handiwork, she frowned as she looked at the (now rather grubby) yellow material. 'I suppose it will do.' Suddenly she looked up, frowning, at Dylan. 'But I don't remember seeing you bringing the insulation in.'

Dylan didn't miss a beat. 'Insulation without aggravation, that's our motto.'

'Well,' sniffed Mrs Furnival-Jones, 'I hope you're going to clear up this mess.'

The 'mess' consisted of one pair of scissors and two tiny pieces of insulation. 'Oh yes,' said a smiling Jez. 'Don't you worry about that.'

Still sniffing, Mrs Furnival-Jones climbed back down the ladder.

As soon as she was out of sight, Dylan turned to Jez. 'So,' he whispered, 'she doesn't want any "mess"?'

'None at all.'

'Well, let's clear it up then.'

Working at the speed of light, they ripped up the newly laid insulation and then hurled it and themselves into Mrs Cummins's attic. There, and with rather more care and attention, they re-laid it. And, as a finishing touch, Dylan left a calling card. *To Mr and Mrs Cummins,* he wrote on a scrap of paper, *may all your winters be warmer.* Below that he added, *LofTec – insulation for the nation.*

They had only just leaped back into Mrs Furnival-Jones's attic when that lady herself reappeared on the ladder. 'Is there a problem?' she shrieked.

Dylan and Jez exchanged a panic-stricken look. Then they ran to the trapdoor. 'Not at all, Mrs Furnival-Jones,' said Dylan, squatting at the top of the ladder, desperately trying to block her view of the attic. Jez, on the other side, did likewise.

Mrs Furnival-Jones sniffed. She wanted proof that there was no mess. 'Have you tidied up?' she demanded, desperately trying to look past them.

Looking slightly green, Jez dangled the small pieces of insulation in front of her. Dylan, smiling manfully, showed her the scissors. 'We were just,' he said, all but shoving her down the ladder, 'coming down.'

Mrs Furnival-Jones sniffed and, reluctantly, climbed back down.

But trouble was already brewing at the other end of the street. James Stratton-Luce had, as was his custom on Fridays, left the office at lunchtime and returned home to criticize his wife. First he objected to her dinner party menu and then to her seating plan. Then, having been rude about the flowers and the hideous dress Eleanor planned to wear, he asked her how her day had been. Normally, he didn't pay the blindest bit of attention to what she said. Today, however, feeling he had been a little harsh, he was prepared to give her one minute of his attention. Time – one had to face facts – was money. But not time spent with Eleanor.

'. . . it would have been helpful,' said Eleanor, after she had been talking for fifty seconds, 'if you'd told me. I really didn't have the cash to spare.'

'Cash?' James hadn't been paying the slightest bit of attention – until he heard the magic word. 'What were you spending spare cash on? And what do you mean by "spare" cash? We don't have any cash to spare.' James was still suffering, terribly, from the bank fiasco. It was Eleanor's private income that kept them in dinner party money.

Eleanor sighed. What was it her mother had told her? 'One year of enchantment, darling – and then a lifetime of etiquette. That's what marriage is.' How right she was, at least about the etiquette bit. They'd never quite fathomed the enchantment.

'James,' she said with another sigh. 'That's what I've been trying to *tell* you. It could have been quails' eggs instead of hens' ones if you hadn't forgotten about the fifty pounds –'

'Fifty pounds? Fifty pounds? What on earth have you been spending fifty pounds on?'

Eleanor lost it. The Sharon in her came out, suddenly and raucously. 'Loft insulation!' she screamed. 'Fucking loft insulation! That's what I've spent fifty pounds on. And I'm bloody glad I did! Now the loft's warm enough for you to fucking sleep in!' Then, Alice band a-quiver, she stormed out of the room.

James, mouth set in a thin, mean line (so nothing's changed there) watched the reverberating door for a moment. Then he headed for the whisky decanter, poured himself a stiff one, downed it in one gulp, and followed his wife out of the room. But that was as far as the following went. While Eleanor went to the kitchen to pour bleach in James's portion of the *garofolato di manzo* (with rocket), James headed for the attic. Five minutes and a short fight with Eleanor later (after which Eleanor added fabric conditioner to James's low-fat milk), he went to call on Mrs Gosling at number three.

Ever polite, Mrs Gosling allowed James to inspect her newly insulated loft, all the while wondering how best to broach the subject of the terrible fights that kept her and Mr Gosling awake at night.

She forgot about broaching when James invited her to inspect her newly denuded loft.

James Stratton-Luce knew a pattern when he saw one – and by the time he had inspected number seventeen he knew exactly what he was up against. Protestations of 'But they were so efficient!' and 'They were utterly charming!' fell by the wayside of the fact that they were also utterly immoral and efficiently dishonest. And, as James made his way down the street, he gathered allies. Mrs Carter-Ross and Mrs Wentworth, initially so captivated by the nice men from LofTec, were now on the warpath. Led by James, they and their neighbours made their angry way down Cranworth Crescent.

Again, it was Georgie who came to the rescue of Jez and Dylan. A clever girl, she realized a) that she had benefited greatly from her sleep, b) that she would be well advised to pass on the bacon roll and c) that the band of Sloane

Rangers she encountered when she went to stretch her legs were, she didn't doubt, after Jez and Dylan.

The Sloanes – braces and Alice bands primed for conflict – seemed to be methodically searching one house after the other on their way down the street. That would indicate, Georgie surmised, that Jez and Dylan were ahead of them – but only just. And it would also indicate that whatever Jez and Dylan were doing, they would shortly be caught in the act.

Georgie had rescued them the day before. Why, she asked herself as she returned to the van to hot-wire the engine, was she taking it upon herself to do so again? Probably, she mused as the van kicked into life, because she was in love.

Mrs Furnival-Jones, although mean, was nothing if not honest. 'Thirty,' she said as she pressed a sixth grubby five-pound note into Dylan's hand. 'The rest, I hope you don't mind, will be in coins.'

Dylan didn't mind.

Jez did. For want of anything better to do, he was staring out of the window. He didn't know exactly what he was expecting to see – but it certainly wasn't Georgie, driving their stolen van, cruising past the house and mouthing the word *run*. At first he didn't, couldn't, believe his eyes. Then, because his eyes made contact with Georgie's, and because she kept repeating her command, he began to believe them. He turned to Dylan. 'Nnn,' he said, meaning *run*.

Dylan looked at him as if he were mad.

'Um,' said Mrs Furnival-Jones, 'let me see . . . I wonder what I've done with those pound coins?'

'Nnn,' said Jez to Dylan.

'What?' mouthed Dylan.

'Run!' yelled Jez, propelling him towards the door.

Out of the corner of his eye, Dylan saw Georgie and the van. They ran back up the stairs, across a couple of lofts, then burst out onto the street.

They were only just in time. Outside, pandemonium ruled over the quiet of Cranworth Crescent. James Stratton-Luce, leading the braying pack of outraged householders, was also bearing down on the van. 'You little bastards!' he screamed. 'Bastards!'

'Not a nice thing,' panted Dylan as he lunged for the passenger door of the van, 'to call a couple of orphans.'

'Quick!' urged Georgie, slipping the van into gear.

They leaped into the van, slamming the door on James Stratton-Luce. 'Bastards!' he yelled again as the van pulled away. Apoplectic with rage, he panted to a halt. Nobody, least of all a couple of bastards, ever got the better of James Stratton-Luce. As the van screeched to the end of the street, he reached into his breast pocket and extracted his electronic personal organizer. Behind him, the rest of the group of householders did likewise. They stood, puffing with exertion, and tapped 'A TO5 OF' into their machines.

Amateurs, they thought, as they did so. Professional con-artists would have blocked out the registration of the van.

Half an hour later, Dave Ray received the shock of his life. His precious van came home to roost. One minute, as he later said to Geoff down at the Rat & Parrot, it wasn't there – the next minute, it was.

Spooky.

Even spookier was the note Dave found folded under the wipers. *Dear Van Owner*, it read. *How sorry I am to have taken your van and probably inconvenienced you terribly. I was rushing back to an ailing relative when my car broke down. Not wishing to be delayed, I took your van and continued on. I have now returned the van with a full tank of petrol and two theatre tickets for Andrew Lloyd Webber's exciting new musical, which I hope will go some way to righting my wrong. Yours sincerely, a friend.*

Babs was ecstatic.

5

Georgie felt she was owed an explanation. Several explanations. As they walked from Dave Ray's house to the tube station, she began to quiz her companions. 'So,' she began, 'you two are compulsive risk takers who thrive on danger – right?'

'Absolutely,' said Dylan.

'But there's something I can't figure out.' Georgie frowned as she watched Dylan and Jez dart into an alley to peel off their Michelin-man outfits. 'You spent a lot of time setting up that computer scam, yes?'

'Yes.' Now down to a tasteless T-shirt and (flared) jeans, Jez was trying to stuff the white jumpsuit into a nearby bin.

'And that pays you tens of thousands of pounds?'

'Well . . .'

'I was there, remember?' said Georgie, stalling Dylan's objection.

'Oh, right.'

'But then you worked just as hard for a few hundred pounds today?'

'Yes.' Jez had spied a skip and was making a beeline for it. Skips were not rubbish bins in their book. They were treasure troves.

'And,' continued Georgie, remembering tea in the gasometer, 'you get free tea and coffee and you even sneak back the cost of your phone calls.'

'Perceptive,' replied Dylan. 'Super perceptive.'

'But why?'

'Because,' explained Dylan, 'we're saving up for that orphans' housing project. And when the cheques clear we'll have raised the necessary funds. Two million pounds.'

'Two million pounds? Gosh.' Georgie frowned. Wasn't that rather over ambitious?

Two million pounds, Dylan was thinking. Enough for a stately home.

Georgie looked at Dylan. A faraway look had come into his eyes, a sort of evangelical dreaminess. The bluster, thought Georgie, was just a cover for the philanthropic zeal underneath. Or was it? 'This,' she said with a sigh, 'is scary. I'm starting to believe you.'

They stopped beside the skip into which Jez had climbed. Georgie watched as he picked out an old seventies radio and a piece of piping. 'This is *totally* bizarre,' she said to herself.

Jez handed his finds to Dylan.

Georgie continued with her inquisition. 'Are you really going to give all the money to an orphans' housing project?'

'Yes,' said Jez. 'We really are.' Well, he thought, they were.

'Do you two ever spend any money?'

'Hmm,' Dylan looked up from the radio and over to Jez. 'In the last three years we've spent . . .'

'Two thousand three hundred and thirty-seven pounds.'

'And,' added Dylan, 'fifty-seven pence.'

'*That*,' said Georgie, 'is anal.'

'You'll never get it to work.' Dylan handed the radio back to Jez.

'I will if I spend enough time on it.'

Dylan shrugged and looked at Georgie. 'He has a degree in the Psychology of Electronics.'

'Psychology of Electronics? What on earth does that mean?'

'It means,' said Jez, 'that I can't get a job.'

Georgie turned to Dylan. 'What about you? What have you got?'

'Dyslexia. It means I can't get a job either.'

Georgie giggled. Then, as she watched Jez fiddle with the radio, a thought occurred to her. 'Toasters,' she announced after a moment. 'Can you fix them?'

'No,' replied Dylan, 'but he can tell you why they wanted to break down.'

'What's the problem with it?' asked Jez.

Georgie shrugged. 'I don't know . . . the bread just doesn't turn to toast.'

'I'd have to see it.'

'Could you come over?'

'Yeah.' Jez affected nonchalance. His heart was racing.
'Sure. 'Course.'

'Later today?'

''Bout six?'

'Brilliant.'

Because she had spent half the day asleep in Dave Ray's
van and not, as planned, engaged in studying, Georgie had
a lot of catching up to do. The trouble was, she also had
a lot to think about.

There were several aspects of Georgie's life about which
she generally kept quiet. She certainly wouldn't dream of
sharing them with people like Jez and Dylan. On the other
hand, she reflected two hours later as she battled (not very
hard) with motor neurones and their specific functions over
the kitchen table, Jez and Dylan seemed oddly trustworthy.
She knew this was a bizarre thing to think about two dyed-in-
the-wool con artists, yet there was an endearing frankness
and honesty about them. And, of course, they were going to
use their ill-gotten gains for an extremely Good Cause.

Good Causes had been uppermost in Georgie's mind for
the last year. One Good Cause in particular. (If you think
you know where this is heading then you're wrong.
Georgie's good cause really is a Good Cause.)

Georgie needed a lot of money – and quickly – for her
Cause. And she wasn't really getting very far in that department. Odd secretarial jobs (some of them very odd) and
occasional bouts of waitressing didn't pay well – and they
played havoc with her studies. And, of course, her social
life.

Ah. Social life. That aspect of Georgie's life was
extremely limited. Her only real social contact was with

her sister, Floss. Her unreal social contact was with Roger – her fiancé.

Dylan and Jez would have been appalled to learn about the fiancé. Georgie was pretty appalled as well, yet Roger did have his merits. Or, at least, one merit: Roger was exceptionally wealthy. And Roger had sworn he would help her with her Good Cause if she would marry him.

It could have been worse. As well as being obscenely rich, Roger was good-looking, kind, charming, well-dressed and well-connected. And young. Glossy magazines with low circulations and high prices held him to be Britain's Most Eligible Bachelor. Socially ambitious mothers (why does Eleanor Stratton-Luce spring to mind?) hurled their plain daughters into his path as he purred past in his Rolls – but Roger wasn't interested. Roger wanted to marry Georgie. Roger had known Georgie since childhood. Roger knew everything about Georgie. And Roger wanted to help Georgie with her Good Cause.

But Roger was a prat.

It was remembering the prat bit that helped Georgie dismiss her fiancé from her mind and concentrate on her motor neurones and, specifically, their functions. She was deeply engrossed in those functions when, at six o'clock precisely, the doorbell rang. Clutching her dressing gown around her, and with an irritated frown, Georgie went to answer it. A Jehovah's Witness, knowing her luck. A man trying to sell her something. A nut.

'Hi,' said Jez as she opened the door. Then, registering her surprise, he added a concerned 'You hadn't forgotten, had you?'

Georgie *had* forgotten. Her suspicion, however, immediately gave way to delight. 'Hi! Come in.'

Jez stepped inside, making nervous, flapping motions with his hands. 'I said I'd come,' he stammered, wincing as he bashed his thigh with the toolbox he was carrying. 'The toaster.'

'Of course.' Georgie grinned and gestured towards the sitting room. 'Thank you.'

Jez walked into the sitting room. No Stratton-Luce eau-de-Sloane here. Georgie's home, he noted with delight, was highly individual. Not, of course, as idiosyncratic as the gasometer, but it certainly had style. It also had a charming, faded elegance that appealed to Jez. It was a room that wore its history well. Then, seeing an ancient globe in the corner below what looked like a family portrait, Jez felt suddenly sad. This, he thought with a pang, is something I'll never have. Legacies from ancestors. Family history.

Forcing a smile, he turned round to Georgie. Then he noticed the dressing gown. 'Have you just got up?'

'No,' she said with a grimace. 'I've been studying.'

'Ah. Medicine.'

'Medicine.'

'Nice place,' said Jez, meaning it.

'Thank you. Shame it's not mine. A friend has lent it to me and my sister.'

'Nice friend.' Jez spied what looked like a family snapshot on the console table beside him. He bent down to look at it. 'This your sister?'

'Mmm,' said Georgie, heading into the kitchen. 'And my little brother.'

The sister, thought Jez, was a bit of a stunner as well. Taller than Georgie, she had long hair and a smile that was very Georgie. She was fair where Georgie was dark and her eyes, unlike Georgie's limpid pools, were a dazzling blue. The brother, however, was very different. His face was slightly puffy and there was something almost Asiatic about his eyes. But he was, like his sisters, smiling broadly.

Jez looked up. A family, he thought. To go with the heirlooms. How wonderful.

Georgie returned with one of those heirlooms. 'It doesn't pop out,' she said, looking doubtful, 'or it won't stay down.'

Jez looked at the toaster and grinned. He wasn't remotely surprised. Then he took it from Georgie's outstretched arms. 'I'm not promising anything, but that's usually a tri-resistal malfunction with the thermostatic control.'

'As simple as that?' teased Georgie.

'Sorry. I'm getting technical.' Jez looked sheepish. 'Sorry.'

Gosh, thought Georgie, he really is uneasy with girls. Regretting the tease, she smiled and gave his arm a reassuring squeeze. 'No, it's okay, I'm joking.'

But Jez was still looking sheepish. 'Dylan says I must never forget the pain that my technical knowledge can cause other people.'

'Dylan says that to you?'

'Yeah. Technically, he's right.'

Georgie laughed. 'You two have a bizarre relationship. How did you meet?'

'Do you really want to know?'

'Is it technical?'

This time it was Jez who laughed. 'No. We were,' he began, 'both unemployed – and over-qualified. We just couldn't seem to find anything . . . anything . . .'

'Legal?'

Jez looked suitably embarrassed. 'No. Anything to . . . to suit our talents.'

'I can understand that,' was Georgie's dry response. 'Anyway, what are Dylan's qualifications?'

'I suppose,' said Jez after a moment, 'you could say he's got a first-class degree from the university of life.'

'Ye-es – he certainly seems streetwise.'

'An entrepreneur is how he puts it.'

'So,' repeated Georgie, 'how did you meet?'

Jez cast his mind back five years to the day that changed both their lives. 'At the gasometer,' he said, surprising Georgie. 'We'd both answered the same ad for casual labour. There was nothing,' he added with a scowl, 'casual about what the foreman wanted us to do. He wanted us to coat every patch of rust on the gasometer with rust paint.'

Georgie wrinkled her nose.

'Which would take us, he reckoned, about three weeks.'

Georgie could understand why Jez and Dylan would have found that an unappealing prospect. Their staying power for jobs appeared to be precisely one day.

'We didn't fancy that,' said Jez unnecessarily, 'so we came up with a scheme to do it in one day.'

(See?)

'How,' said Georgie, 'could you possibly do it in one day?'

Jez grinned. 'Easy. Rather than use the scaffolding, we stayed on the ground and used a catapult.'

'A catapult?'

'Yes. Lateral thinking . . . y'know . . . like how the Egyptians built the pyramids.'

Georgie was lost. 'They built the pyramids by catapult?'

'No.' Jez shuffled from one foot to the other. 'It's just . . . like, there are several ways of solving problems and you have to look for the easiest.'

Georgie could see that.

'So, rather than construct scaffolding, climb up the gas-ometer and paint every single spot with a brush, we used dollops of paint and a catapult.'

Georgie burst out laughing. 'And it worked?'

'A treat. Except,' added Jez, 'when the foreman came back three weeks later, it was to tell us that the firm had gone bust and he couldn't pay us.'

'Oh.'

'Which meant that neither of us could pay our rent.'

'Ah.'

'Which meant that we had to look for somewhere else to live.'

Georgie grinned. 'Which meant that you didn't have to look very far?'

'No. We'd already found the key to the inside of the gasometer and . . .' fearing that he was boring Georgie, Jez shrugged and looked down at the toaster. 'Well, the rest is history.'

'How long ago was that?'

'Oh . . .'bout five years.'

'And you've been together ever since?'

Jez looked alarmed. 'We're not . . .'

'I know.' Georgie looked embarrassed. 'What I mean is, that you've been living and working together ever since then?'

'Yes.'

'Doesn't that get a bit claustrophobic? I mean, don't you ever get fed up of each other?'

Jez looked extremely surprised. 'We're friends, Georgie.' Struggling to find the correct words, he looked into the mid-distance. 'I mean . . . well . . . we don't . . . that is, I don't . . . I mean,' he finished, 'we don't need anybody else.'

As soon as he uttered the words, he regretted them. Damn, he thought, catching the expression on Georgie's face. 'What I mean,' he stammered, 'is that we don't need –'

'Am I disturbing something?' The strong, cut-glass vowels cut straight through Jez's confused mutterings. Both he and Georgie looked up in surprise.

The girl from the photograph was standing in the doorway wearing Georgie's smile and, beneath it, a beautifully cut cream linen suit.

Georgie grinned, the look of alarm giving way to one of affection. 'No – nothing. This,' she said, 'is Jez. And Jez, this is Floss, my younger sister.'

Feeling awkward and suddenly shy, Jez stood up and shook hands. 'Er . . . hello.'

'Pleased to meet you,' said Floss.

Mesmerized by the double vision of beauty, Jez couldn't think what to say next. He looked down at the toaster. 'Er . . . it's a very interesting model.'

'Sorry?' Floss was politely puzzled.

'The Morphy Richards BB 80. Your toaster.'

'Oh,' said Floss. 'Right.' Then, grinning, 'Yes. A lot of people have told us that.'

Jez felt even more awkward.

Floss flashed him a dazzling smile and then touched Georgie on the shoulder. 'Well, I'd better be off. Night shift,' she said with a grimace.

'Night shift?' said Jez when she had closed the door. Floss didn't look like a night shift sort of person – especially dressed like that.

'She works as a receptionist in a hotel some nights. Extra cash.'

'Ah.' Jez nodded in understanding. Night shift, in his

experience, meant security work or shelling peas in a factory. Pea shellers didn't wear smart tailored suits and pearls. Receptionists, obviously, did. Jez smiled over to Georgie. 'You work a lot in your family, don't you?'

A fleeting, pained look flashed across Georgie's features. 'We have to.' Then, smiling, she added, 'But we do play as well.'

Oh good, thought Jez.

'Which reminds me.' Georgie looked at her watch and stood up. 'I've got to get ready. Would you excuse me a minute?'

Jez nodded and quickly bowed his head over the toaster. Damn, he thought. Then he reminded himself that he was, after all, only the toaster man. People like Georgie didn't go out to play with people like him.

Twenty minutes later the toaster was mended and Georgie still hadn't returned. Jez's acquaintance with the opposite sex had been sporadic and not particularly broad – and certainly not extensive enough to have instilled into him that the female *minute* to *get ready* was a wholly elastic term. He sat where he was for a moment, wondering if Georgie was all right. Judging by the toaster, she was obviously accident-prone. Supposing she had fallen at the top of the stairs? What if she had drowned in the bath?

She hadn't. She had, however, made extremely good use of her twenty minutes. The fresh gamine who had earlier left the room in a dressing gown now returned a sophisticated woman in a ball gown. She was almost unrecognizable.

'My God!' stammered Jez as she shimmered into the room. 'You look . . . you look . . .'

Although inherently modest, Georgie wasn't averse to a

touch of flattery. 'Oh,' she said with a grin, 'it's just something I threw on. So,' she added, 'did you get it working?'

'What?' Jez couldn't take his eyes off her. The slicked-back hair, the bright-red lips, the touch of blusher on her cheeks and the eye shadow that enhanced those beautiful dark eyes – the transformation was astonishing. And as for the dress . . .

'The Morphy,' said Georgie, pointing with a newly painted nail. 'The toaster.'

Jez could only manage a nod.

Georgie looked as if all her Christmases had come at once. 'Thank you *so* much,' she beamed.

It's only a toaster, thought Jez. And, he remembered, I'm only the toaster man. This gorgeous apparition is not for me. 'Well,' he said with a bright, forced smile. 'I'd better go.'

Georgie looked at her watch again – a different watch, Jez noticed. 'Yes,' she said absently. 'Me, too.' Then she escorted Jez to the front door. 'Thanks, Jez,' she said as she opened it. 'You're wonderful.'

Jez went pink.

'I'm wonderful,' he whispered to himself as he walked into the street.

And then Jez deliberately sabotaged his wonderfulness. He was halfway down the street when the thought occurred to him – and once it was there it wouldn't budge. It grew and, despite the fact that it was torturing him, he knew he would have to act on it.

Jez crossed the road and retraced his steps until he was directly opposite Georgie's house. Then he lowered himself behind a parked car and waited.

Ten agonizing minutes passed, minutes that brought

heavy rain, that soaked Jez to the skin and increased his misery. Why on earth, he wondered, am I doing this to myself?

When it happened it was worse, much worse than he had thought. The car was a gleaming Rolls-Royce. The driver was a uniformed chauffeur. And the man who emerged from the back seat holding one of the largest bunches of flowers Jez had ever seen was tall, dark, young and handsome.

Jez thought he would throw up. He very nearly did when Georgie opened the door and kissed the man on the lips.

6

Jez decided that there was only one thing for it: he must
forget all about Georgie. She, obviously, would forget all
about him. Maybe she already had.

As far as Jez was concerned, the twenty-four hours after
the shivering-in-the-rain episode passed agonizingly slowly.
As far as things like plot were concerned, however, they
skipped along nicely. In fact, they disappeared altogether.

In the Gasometer

Aware that people often went for solitary walks in the rain
to indulge their misery, Jez had gone for a solitary walk

in the rain to indulge his misery. When he returned to the gasometer, Dylan was sitting cross-legged in the middle of the floor surrounded by life-sized plastic blow-up dolls.

Jez felt suddenly better about Georgie. However miserable she made him feel, she could never reduce him to *this*. 'Sorry,' he said from the doorway, 'I didn't realize you were this lonely. I missed the signs.' Then, as he approached Dylan, he realized his friend was shaking with hysterical laughter and not tears. He was also red in the face from too much doll-blowing.

'Where on earth did these come from?' said Jez, also beginning to laugh.

Dylan looked up and grinned. 'Don't you remember? "Never a wrinkle, never a crease, make it thin or make it obese"?'

'Yes! Of course. Blenson's Pack-Away Mannequins!'

'And so useful.' Dylan giggled again at the dolls. They were identical and all wore expressions of extreme surprise: their mouths were wide open (no need to go into the reasons for that) and their eyelashes batted up and down at the slightest vibration.

Jez sat down on the fluorescent beanbag beside Dylan. The doll nearest to him batted her eyelashes like fury and fell from a sitting position into a dead faint. Jez picked her up. 'Shall we dance?' he invited.

Not being designed to participate in vertical activities, the doll looked surprised. Undaunted, Jez clasped her to him and, to the strains of Burt Bacharach, waltzed around with her. Laughing uproariously, Dylan looked on for a moment and then gallantly offered his hand to the doll nearest him. Rather than looking surprised, she seemed to shrink from him. Perturbed, Dylan leaned closer and turned her over. In protest, she expelled a blast of air. 'Ah,' said Dylan, nodding to himself. 'Her valve's open.'

'What?' enquired the waltzing Jez.

'Nothing,' said Dylan, administering the kiss (or blow) of life. Then, dancing partner restored to working order, he whirled her around the floor.

'Two left feet,' he yelled over to Jez.

'I don't think the feet are the most important bits.'

'No, probably not. D'you think,' he shouted over Burt's croons, 'someone lost their girlie store licence?'

'Expect so,' replied Jez, executing a particularly nifty little *pas de deux*. 'Should we keep them?'

'Oh, I think so,' said Dylan, throwing his partner over his shoulder. 'You never know when they might come in useful.'

No, indeed. You never know.

In Georgie's House

'God, I'm knackered.'

Floss looked on in sympathy as Georgie threw herself onto the sofa and closed her eyes.

'You're doing too much,' she said.

Georgie shook her head. 'I'll be okay.'

'We're almost there with this month's payment,' said Floss with a smile.

Georgie opened her eyes and stared balefully at her sister. 'It feels like we're just keeping a sinking ship afloat. Unless we get enough money to actually buy the foundation outright, I really think we're wasting our time.'

Money, thought Floss. A vision of Roger floated in front of her. 'How was the ball?' she asked.

Georgie groaned. 'Too posh.'

Floss giggled. Then, suddenly serious, she sat down beside Georgie. 'D'you think Roger'll . . . ?'

Georgie held up a hand. 'I don't know, Floss. I don't want to force him. It would seem so mercenary.'

'And that's a word unfamiliar to Roger, is it?'

'*Please*, Floss.'

'Oh, all right.' Floss knew when to change the subject. 'Who was that guy,' she asked suddenly, 'you know, the "toast master"?'

Georgie smiled. 'Just some man with a mission.'

'And . . . ?'

'And nothing.'

Oh.

Number One, Cranworth Crescent

'Eighteen hours!' bellowed James Stratton-Luce. 'Eighteen hours you've known about this! Surely tracing a car number plate is not a problem even for someone of your intelligence!'

Police Constable Camilla Cash stared in disbelief at the man in front of her. Partly because she was called Camilla and partly because she trod the smart beat of Holland Park, she had encountered her fair share of socially aspirant, emotionally illiterate, racist, prejudiced, sexually incompetent johnny-come-lately little people. But this man took the biscuit. He was glaring at her through ice-blue eyes. Camilla glared back. Mindful of her job and trying not to sound as haughty as the man's appalling wife, she declared, 'We have rather a lot of conflicting information, sir.' The 'sir' sounded, and was meant to sound, like an insult.

James wasn't going to be intimidated by some jumped-up constable. 'What,' he barked, 'do you mean by that?'

Camilla pulled her notes from her breast pocket and looked at James. 'Well,' she said with her perfect elocution, 'we know that one of the suspects is English. But the other chap,' she said, reading her notes, 'is either Dutch, Australian, Belgian or Welsh. And,' she finished with a triumphant smirk, 'one of your neighbours has been claiming that one of them is black. Now, what do you make of that?'

James was sorely tempted to lash out at the ghastly woman. Three reasons prevented him from doing so. One was that it was frightfully common to tussle with the police. Another was that he made it a policy never to hit women. The third was that he knew a bolt to the bathroom was, yet again, imminent. James hadn't been feeling terribly well that day. James, in fact, had been violently ill all through the previous night and for much of that morning. In the normal course of events, this would have been Eleanor's fault but, annoyingly, he couldn't blame her this time. He hadn't eaten any of her revolting food last night. He had contented himself with a few sips of milk.

James didn't deign to reply to Camilla's sneering question. Instead, with as much dignity as he could muster, he made for the door, turning, as he exited, to declare, 'My wife will show you out.'

But Eleanor had disappeared. Eleanor was, in fact, in the upstairs lav syringing laxative into James's anti-diarrhoea medicine. Alice band askew, hair dishevelled and eyes unfocused, she cackled as she did so. This, she thought, would teach him a lesson. This would really give the bastard something to complain about. And no longer would the medicine live up to its legend. There was no way it could now 'Stop the runs from your family's tums'.

Now who could possibly have thought up a line like that?

In Dave Ray's House

Babs was nearly ready. Her meticulous preparations were nearing completion. Mervyn had been to 'do' her highlights (more accurately, to deposit a bucket of peroxide on her brittle beehive). Deirdre from the make-up counter had called round to help her with her face, and, that morning, Babs and Trixie had combed the high street for a suitable outfit.

And now all the various elements of Babs's *toilette* were coming together in, appropriately enough, her toilet. And it was *her* toilet. Make no mistake about that. You could tell that by the pansy-petalled placard on the outside of the door. BABS'S BOUDOIR it boasted in swirly pink letters. Dave had his own bog down the corridor.

A little more eyeliner, thought Babs as she peered into the pink-tinged mirror. A dab more lipstick. A spot more rouge. And should she be wearing longer eyelashes? After all, you never knew who might be at the theatre. Lord Lloyd-Webber himself? Joan Collins? You never knew.

Satisfied, indeed delighted, with her appearance, Babs emerged from her boudoir and made her delicate way down-stairs. Her husband, while not the most observant nor indeed complimentary of men, would be bowled over.

Because she was going to town, Babs had really gone to town.

She lingered at the foot of the stairs and draped herself coquettishly round the bottom banister. Rather like Lana Turner in that film, she reckoned.

And then she cooed over to her Clark Gable that she was ready.

Dave didn't even look up. Throwing the *Racing Post* onto the floor, he stood up and fished for his van keys. Then his manly chiselled lips parted and he uttered his love cry: 'What kept you, you dozy old cow?'

Ouch.

Jez's misery returned. Most people would probably feel pretty miserable after dancing with a blow-up doll to the strains of Burt Bacharach, as Jez had just done, but that was not why Jez was gloomy. He was thinking about Georgie again. Not surprising, really, considering he was in the process of driving Dylan to the West End so that he could go to the theatre with her.

Jez's one consolation was that Georgie had told Dylan she would meet him at the theatre, not at her house.

'So,' said Jez, as he turned into Shaftesbury Avenue. 'You'll be back around eleven, then?'

Dylan shot him an old-fashioned look. 'Am I missing something or are you my mother?'

'Well,' shrugged Jez. 'The show finishes at ten-thirty . . .'

'Yeah. Maybe I'll be back at eleven. Maybe I won't.'

Jez sighed and pulled over as they reached the theatre. 'You're going to try it on with Georgie, aren't you?'

Dylan smirked and hummed a bar from 'Hey There, Georgie Girl'.

'Oh, get out.' For the first time in five years, Jez was seriously annoyed with Dylan. What was it Georgie had asked? Don't you ever get fed up with each other? And Jez had said no. Huh.

Dylan opened the door and leaped out of the car. Then, suddenly, he turned back and leaned towards his friend. 'Jez,' he said, his face now a picture of affectionate concern, 'we can change places if you like. If you're really upset about this then you can do the theatre and I'll get the laptop back.'

Jez flew into a blind panic. Sitting knee to knee with Georgie in a cramped theatre? What would he talk about? What would he do? 'No,' he said, 'but thanks for the offer.' Then, smiling up at his friend, he added, 'Anyway, you're crap at lock breaking and I hate musicals.'

Dylan grinned. 'True.' He didn't have the heart to tell Jez that everyone hated musicals. He held up a hand in salute. 'Good luck.'

'See you,' replied Jez, 'at eleven.'

Dylan sauntered into the foyer of the theatre, one eye scouting for Georgie, the other at his reflection in the mirrored wall. Several women – and a few men – cast covert, appraising glances in his direction. Dylan carried himself with such confidence, exuded such magnetism that it was difficult to ignore his presence. None of the people who looked at him could have guessed that the self-possession, the vanity and the air of calm assurance was a cover for terminal insecurity. Dylan himself didn't even know that. His powers of self-analysis were not great. All he knew about himself was that he always had to keep moving, always had to be on the go. Sometimes it was rather wearing.

After ten minutes, Georgie had still not appeared. Nor, for that matter, had the owner of A TO5 OF and his lady wife. Dylan began to fret.

'Dylan?'

'Georgie!' He hadn't noticed her under the floppy hat. Grinning broadly, he bent down to peck her on the cheek. 'I was beginning to think you weren't coming.' This was a most un-Dylan-like thing to say. He must have been worried.

'Of course I was going to come.' Georgie fixed him with an impish smile. 'You owe me seventy-five pounds.'

'Ah.' Dylan was taken aback. 'I didn't think nice English girls were so upfront.'

'I don't remember ever saying I was nice.'

'No.' Dylan reached for her arm. 'It was me who said that. Come on, babe, that was the first bell. We'd better get to our seats.'

'By the way,' said Georgie, as they threaded their way up to the dress circle, 'you never asked me if I liked musicals.'

'Do you?'

'No.'

'Good. Nor do I. Nobody does, do they?' With that, Dylan ushered her into the auditorium.

'Here,' he said as they sat down, 'is your seventy-five bucks.'

Georgie took the proffered notes. 'Thank you. Dylan . . . ?'

She was interrupted by the loudspeaker. 'Andrew Lloyd Webber's riveting new musical,' boomed a flat voice, 'will be starting in three minutes.' It was unclear whether this announcement was a promise or a threat.

'Dylan?'

'Mmm?'

'Can I ask you how long you've been in England?'

'Sure, babe.'

Silence. Georgie looked at Dylan. He responded with a cheeky grin.

'How long,' she sighed, 'have you been in England?'

'Five years.'

'And you still say *bucks* and *babe*?'

Dylan nodded, peering over the balustrade to the stalls below them. 'Sad, isn't it?' He flashed her a quick smile. 'Okay, I'll try it in English ... Hello me ol' copper, fancy some quids and apples and pears ... ?'

Georgie winced. As Cockney accents went, this had to be the worst she'd ever heard. 'Thank you,' she said, 'for trying.'

'Sound of Bow Bells,' continued Dylan, 'never on your nelly.'

'Thank you.'

Another smile, crooked this time. 'That's okay, me ol' china tea cup.'

'I never thought I'd say this, but ... American, please.'

Dylan shrugged. 'Okay, chipper.' Then, looking over the balustrade again, he hit his knee on the opera glasses in front of them. 'Ah!' he said, looking down. 'The very thing.'

'You'll need twenty pee.'

'No, I won't.' Dylan reached into his breast pocket.

No, thought Georgie, remembering who he was, you probably won't.

He didn't. He extracted a thin plastic card from his pocket and attacked the opera glasses holder with it. Ten seconds later – and in defiance of Jez's claim that he was crap at picking locks – the holder snapped open, releasing the opera glasses.

Dylan smiled in satisfaction and, glasses raised, scoured the stalls below them.

'Oh my God!' he said after a moment.

'What?'

'They've arrived.'

Georgie looked puzzled. 'I thought that was the plan.'

'It was. I just didn't know what Mrs Van planned to wear. Here,' he said, handing her the glasses. 'Take a peek.'

Georgie focused on the man who had stolen her bag two days previously. He looks, she thought, exactly the same. Stupid and unkind. He also looks as if he really doesn't want to be here.

Then she turned the glasses on his wife and realized why. 'Oh,' she squealed. 'Oh . . . my . . . God!'

Below her, Babs was aware of the admiring glances coming her way. There were, if she was honest, rather more of them than she had anticipated. She found them, if truth be told, rather unnerving. She really wasn't, bearing in mind that she was married to Dave, used to being the centre of attention. And she had, she realized, gone rather over the top.

Babs's outfit was themed to compliment the show; planned, unselfishly, as a tribute to Lord Andrew and, selfishly, to steal Joan Collins's thunder. (Joan, had she been there and not on a yacht in the Mediterranean, would have passed unnoticed. She wouldn't even have made the orchestra, let alone played second fiddle to Babs.)

For Babs, resplendent in shocking pink, was dressed as

a toy poodle. She had actually owned a toy poodle – Fluffy – in the past, so she knew what she was doing. The beehive, coaxed forward by Mervyn, was now a glorious powder puff, a heavenly cloudburst of candyfloss hovering above her forehead. The dainty wrists sported matching cuffs, the neck a complimentary ruff and, unhappily invisible to the auditorium at large, the little feet nestled in pink bootees with a fluffy white border at the ankle. The rest of Babs (and there was quite a lot of Babs) was clad in a clinging, fluorescent pink catsuit.

It was the catsuit that had posed the biggest problem for Babs. Would Andrew, she had agonized, be offended at her wearing such an item to a show called *Dogs*?

Above the pitiable Babs, Georgie had collapsed in a fit of helpless giggles. Beside her, Dylan had recovered from his own hysterics and, although still grinning, was now occupied with his mobile phone. There was serious work to be done.

Jez answered the phone after two rings. 'Dylan?'

'Yeah. We're all set. They've arrived.'

In the car on Shaftesbury Avenue, Jez breathed a sigh of relief. 'Okay, I'll be off then. Er . . . see you at eleven?'

But the phone had gone dead.

Twenty minutes later, Jez pulled up outside Dave Ray's house. The place, he was relieved to see, was in total darkness and the lock on the front door, he was even more relieved to discover, was child's play to pick. Even Dylan could have managed it.

Jez slipped into the house and, keeping one hand cupped over the beam, switched on his torch. The sitting room, he decided, would be the best bet.

Jez switched off the torch altogether when he entered

the room. The street lamps gave enough light for him to see. More importantly, he didn't think he could face this monumental crime against taste in all its fluorescent glory. The glimpse through the window the other evening had been quite enough.

Jez began to root around for his computer, occasionally switching on the torch for guidance. The beam, as it fell on the faux Louis XV bookcase beside the crystal swan in the corner, illuminated a pile of magazines. *Guns and Ammo*, Jez noted. *Security World*. *Soap Stars' Hairstyles*. He wondered what sort of conversations Mr and Mrs Van had with each other.

Then, on the velour sofa, he saw his computer. It still bore traces of fried chicken fingerprints and looked as if it had been tossed aside like an out-of-favour toy. It looked as if Mr Van had made no progress in deciphering its secrets. Which was, thought Jez, just as well.

He picked up the machine and, half the job done, crept out of the house and then back to the car.

The other half of the job would leave the police in absolutely no doubt whatsoever that the owner of A TO5 OF was the perpetrator of the loft insulation scam. Jez returned from the car with a roll of insulation material and a pile of empty insulation bags. Pondering on the best place to secrete them, he looked out the kitchen window and into the back garden. The shed. Perfect.

Walking back though the sitting room to the front door, Jez caught sight of the video recorder beneath the giant TV. His eyes lit up as he saw the timer flashing. He grinned quietly. A little mischief was in order; a little calling card should be left. He deserved a little fun. Kneeling down in front of the video, he noted the time and channel of the programme to be recorded. Then he picked up a copy of *Radio Times*. 'Aha,' he said with satisfaction as his finger stopped on *Blind Date*. Mrs Van's choice, he mused. Poor Mr Van. What, he wondered would they *both* like to watch? What would provide them with a spot of loving togetherness?

Jez's eyes lit up when he saw the listing for *Dispatches* on Channel Four. '*Dispatches*,' he read, 'investigates the impact of microchip technology on the longterm storage of wheat reserves in northern Russia.'

'Now that,' said Jez to himself, 'is what I call entertainment.'

Kneeling again in front of the video, he rearranged the timer to the satisfaction, he didn't doubt, of both the lady and the gentleman of the house.

Then he reached for the phone. 'International directories?' he asked after a moment. 'Yes. Could you please get me the speaking clock in São Paulo? Yes,' he repeated a few seconds later. 'Thank you.' Just as well, he said to himself, that it was he, not Dylan, doing the Van visiting. Dylan would never be able to remember a twenty-digit number.

Jez replaced the receiver, picked it up again, and dialled São Paulo. When the Portuguese speaking clock obligingly answered, Jez grinned and replaced the receiver. But this time he placed it beside, not on, the base. Mr and Mrs Van, he knew, had a burning desire to be kept permanently abreast of Brazilian timescale developments. It was their highly expensive and secret little vice.

Jez stood up and looked again round the hideous room. What now? What other little delights to inflict on the Vans? On the wall opposite the plastic brick fireplace, he noted an array of nasty little pictures – at least thirty of them. They were all, he saw with glee, painstakingly arranged in straight lines and in perfect symmetry. Jez walked to the wall and then proceeded to rearrange every picture, putting them upside down and slightly off-kilter. Then, stepping back, he frowned. He had probably done the Vans a favour. Now that the pictures were upside down they didn't look quite so nasty. Still, at least they were crooked.

Then the light in the hall went on.

The musical had barely begun when the thought occurred to Dave Ray. Supposing, he thought, just supposing? After all, being a criminal himself, he knew every trick in the book. Best to make absolutely sure.

He looked around him. The entire audience, with the notable exception of the raptly attentive Babs, had fallen asleep. Not even the cacophony of howling and whining from the stage could keep them awake. Nodding in satisfaction, Dave rose to his feet and edged his way over the prone bodies beside him to the aisle. Then he walked briskly towards the foyer and the bank of telephones in the corner.

Dylan and Georgie, fast asleep in the dress circle, were unaware of his departure.

Geoff was, as Dave knew he would be, in the Rat & Parrot round the corner from his house. 'Geoff,' he said once he had him on the line, 'I want you to do something for me . . . Y'know those tickets someone gave us? Yeah, yeah . . . no, it wasn't very kind, actually, but that's not the point. I want to know if it's the old theatre trick. Could you go and check on the house?' Then, after a moment, he added, 'Ta, mate. I owe you one.'

*   *   *

That was how, a few seconds after the hall light went on, the bank of multi-coloured fluorescent lights illuminated the sitting room and Jez found himself staring at a man he didn't know (Geoff, of course). For a moment he did a passable imitation of a rabbit transfixed in the headlights of an approaching car. Then he said, 'Hi.' And bolted for the back door.

He made it outside and to the garden wall before Geoff caught up with him. As Jez launched himself at the top of the wall, he felt hands flailing around his legs and grappling at the voluminous material of his trousers (Jez was wearing his flares again). It was those very trousers that proved his salvation. Eat your heart out, drainpipe jeans, thought Jez as he managed to haul his torso onto the top of the wall. The grubby, chubby tobacco-stained hands were now gripping rather then grappling. They thought they were winning – but they didn't anticipate that Jez would undo his belt, unzip his fly and abandon the trousers altogether, doing himself, and mankind, an immense favour. Flares, he grudgingly admitted to himself as he sailed over the wall, were never going to make a concerted comeback. And nor, to this particular neck of the woods, was Jez. He leaped to his feet and disappeared into the night.

On the other side of the wall, there was no longer any resistance to Geoff's pulling. Geoff flew backwards to the ground, decapitating, as he fell, Babs's favourite gnome.

Later that evening, Jez's misery returned. He was still, at eleven o'clock, alone in the gasometer. He was still alone at eleven-thirty. And when the grandfather clock in the corner chimed midnight, he was still alone. Unless, of course, you counted the blow-up dolls. Oblivious to both

Jez and the passing of time, they were lolling around on bean bags.

'Where are you?' said Jez to himself, hugging his knees to his chest. 'You're going to sleep with her, aren't you? You're going to *romance* her at that nightclub. Then you're going to sleep with her.'

The thought was too much for Jez. Galvanizing himself into action, he leaped up from the sofa and shot out of the gasometer.

Georgie Makes a Mistake

'It's just,' said Georgie as she rammed her floppy hat further down onto her head, 'that I'm not that keen on nightclubs.'

'Don't be a Jez,' countered Dylan with a wolfish smile. 'It's fun.'

Georgie sighed. 'I'm not wearing the right clothes. I'm tired. And I hate loud music.' Did this man, she wondered, have the hide of a rhinoceros? 'And,' she added rather nastily, 'I didn't enjoy the show one little bit.'

''Course you didn't. That's why,' he persisted, 'you have to come to the nightclub. It'll be the perfect contrast. It'll be great.'

'Look, Dylan . . .'

'Georgie.' Dylan stepped closer. 'You're beautiful, you're sexy and you're a bit troubled. This,' he gestured at the flickering neon, 'will make you feel better.'

'Why do you think I'm troubled?'

'I'm quite emotionally sensitive.'

Georgie snorted. 'You're the least emotionally sensitive person I've ever met.'

But Dylan was still smiling at her. Georgie couldn't help smiling back. And she couldn't find it in her to resist further. She let Dylan escort her to the front of the queue and into the nightclub.

Camilla Makes an Arrest

It wasn't really her territory, but Camilla would have done anything to get the residents of Cranworth Crescent out of her hair once and for all. She was even prepared to venture south of the river. Which was why, at half-past eleven, she found herself in the unfamiliar and alarming environs of Wandsworth. No place, she mused with distaste, for the police to venture at night. Still, one had to take the rough with the smooth.

'Mr Ray,' said Camilla, as soon as she had stopped reeling from the shock of the sitting room, 'you are under arrest.'

Dave laughed. 'What for? You won't be able to pin anything on me.' Not, really, the brightest of remarks.

'No?'

'No. I'm telling you, *I'm* the one that's been burgled.'

'So you keep telling me.'

'And you're not going to do anything about it?'

'As I'm in Wandsworth, no.' Then Camilla sighed and extracted her notebook from her breast pocket. 'Mr Ray. I'm arresting you on suspicion of extortion and laying loft insulation under false pretences.'

'*Loft* insulation?' Dave was poleaxed. Babs, too, seemed a little alarmed. But then anyone dressed as a poodle, surmised Camilla, has a right to look alarmed.

'Look,' repeated Dave, *I'm* the one who's been burgled.'

Camilla sighed again. 'Mr Ray, the only "proof" of burglary is that someone stopped your video taping *Blind Date.*'

'Bastards,' seethed Babs through pursed lips. 'Bastards!'

'Shut it,' snapped Dave.

Then Camilla's colleague came into the room carrying a pair of trousers and the roll of insulation that Jez had left in the shed. 'Oh, yes,' said Camilla, arching an eyebrow. 'More proof.'

'But what about the pictures?' screamed Babs as Camilla stepped forward to handcuff her husband.

'Very nice, Mrs Ray,' lied Camilla. 'Very nice indeed.'

Dylan Makes a Move

Georgie felt she was in a nightmare rather than a nightclub. The music was unbearably loud, the people were unpleasantly sweaty and the flashing neon lights were already giving her a headache.

Dylan didn't appear to notice. For him, this was nirvana rather than a nightclub. And he knew that Georgie would soon be in heaven. True, she was looking slightly dazed at the moment – but in another moment she would find herself melting into his arms. She was about to experience his famous and irresistible seduction routine.

This routine was well practised. It basically involved requesting the DJ to play some Barry White and then, hips snaking and eyes shining, accompanying the words of the master of slush.

'Why,' crooned Dylan in a husky, sex-laden drawl as he

wriggled up to Georgie, 'you look so good tonight, I want to pleasure you with my tongue.'

'I need some air,' said Georgie, and bolted from the club.

Jez Makes a Move

Georgie ran smack into Jez. His misery, combined with his knowledge of Dylan's famous and irresistible seduction routine, had taken him to the street outside the club. He knew it would only be a matter of time before Georgie bolted. He hoped that it would look like nothing more than a happy coincidence that he just happened to be lurking there. He was wrong.

'Hello!' Georgie was astonished. But then again, she thought as she recovered from her shock, maybe I'm not. 'This *is* a surprise.'

'Er . . . yes, isn't it?'

'What are you doing here?' Georgie looked into Jez's eyes and then, giggling, down to his boxer shorts. 'Is it scouts' night?'

Jez had forgotten about the trouser episode and looked down, embarrassed, at his bare legs. 'Er . . . no,' he said with a rueful grin, 'I was just passing and . . . are you okay?' Suddenly he noticed how shattered Georgie looked.

She heaved a sigh. 'Yes. I'm all right.'

Jez looked at her in concern. 'Did he,' he whispered as he stepped closer, 'try to pleasure you with his tongue?'

Georgie wasn't sure whether she was amused or angry. 'Is it,' she said, looking into Jez's eyes, 'that obvious?'

Jez shrugged. Then, with a tentative smile, he offered to walk Georgie home. Georgie accepted.

'It's a kind of compulsion with him,' Jez said as they fell into step together. 'He wants to exchange fluids with everyone he meets. That,' he explained, 'is why we've never had a dog.'

Georgie grinned. Beside her, Jez fidgeted.

'Do you like nightclubs?' he asked. She didn't, he reckoned, look the clubbing sort.

Georgie shuddered. 'I hate them.'

'Me, too.' Jez was positively fumbling now. 'The . . . the decibel level can reach –'

'Jez.' Georgie forcibly stopped him in his tracks and looked straight into his eyes. 'Jez,' she urged, 'you don't have to be nervous with me.' Then, in a softer voice, 'It's okay, you know.'

Jez didn't reply for a moment. When he did, he surprised the life out of Georgie. 'Would you like,' he asked, 'to come to the roof of the gasometer?'

'The gasometer?'

'Yeah . . . y'know . . .'

Georgie looked up at the full moon and the shining stars. 'Yes. I'd love to.'

The gasometer at night was a special place; Jez's special place. It was here he would come when he wanted to be alone with his thoughts, here he would come at night to ponder the universe and his place in it. And it was here, on a very few occasions, that he had brought a girl.

Georgie was in raptures. The climb up the inspection ladder had, admittedly, been about as exhausting as the nightclub – but the rewards were infinitely greater. In the centre of the flat roof was a pool of rainwater, perfect and round and like a small lake. The idyllic impression was further enhanced by the ducks and the geese paddling in the water, by the greenery that had started growing and by the sediment around the water creating, in the dark, the impression of a beach.

But it was the view that really took Georgie's breath away. The whole of London was spread out before them, sparkling and still, bathed in its own twinkling lights and in that of the constellations above them. It was as if they were on top of the world.

'Oh,' she breathed as they sat at the edge. 'It's beautiful.'

'Mmm.' Jez stared out into the night sky. 'No one ever comes up here apart from me.'

'Really? Why?'

Jez leaned forward, away from Georgie. 'I don't know. I invited a person up here once. Y'know . . . "Come up to the roof tonight, there's a couple of mallards about to roost", but they just seemed to get nervous.'

Georgie found herself laughing. Jez, apart from anything else, was so *sweet*. And why, she wondered, as she looked at his profile, did he think he was an ugly duckling? She looked over at him. 'You're very funny,' she said, meaning it. 'You know that?' Funny nice, she meant. Not funny laughable. She hoped he knew that. Then, when he didn't reply, her look changed to one of concern. Jez, she noticed, was looking uncomfortable again. 'What's the matter?' she asked.

'Nothing. I'm fine.'

'You're not,' challenged Georgie.

'No.' Jez grinned and scratched his neck. 'I'm not.'

'Show me.'

Jez turned to her. He looked, she thought, distinctly miserable. 'We got a bulk shipment,' he began, pointing to his chest, 'of these T-shirts a while back. From a multi-entry competition.'

'I beg your pardon?'

'"Give your cat Glitz",' quoted Jez, '"it's like dining at the Ritz".'

Georgie looked at the T-shirt bearing that legend. 'Ah,' she said, understanding at last, 'and it hurts you?'

'The label,' said Jez, scratching his neck, 'is itchy.'

'The label,' repeated Georgie, 'is itchy.' As she spoke, she lifted the lock of Jez's hair that spilled over his collar and pulled at the offending T-shirt. 'I really need,' she breathed as she looked at the label, 'a pair of scissors.'

Jez pulled a penknife out of his shirt pocket. If Georgie was surprised, she didn't show it. She smiled her thanks and addressed herself, once again, to the nape of his neck.

Jez shivered as Georgie cut out the label. The touch of her hand at the back of his neck was, to put it mildly, incredibly erotic. He turned to look at Georgie. Her expression, unlike his, was inscrutable. He couldn't tell what she was feeling.

But Georgie knew exactly what she was feeling. Betrayal. Suddenly she stood up. 'I should go,' she said, avoiding Jez's questioning look.

'Yes,' replied Jez, staring into the firmament above.

'It's a lovely place,' said Georgie. 'Special.'

'Yeah.'

But the moment was lost and, sensing that she had ruined it, Georgie left.

It was a good ten minutes before Jez, feeling utterly miserable, descended from the roof. He reached ground level and opened the door to the home that he shared with

Dylan. Out of habit, he walked over to Dylan's greenhouse to check that he was all right.

Dressed in one of his impeccable suits, Dylan was splayed out on his bed. He was, as usual, alone. And, as usual, he was sucking his thumb. Typical, thought Jez. All talk and no trouser. Then, still in his boxer shorts, he padded across the silent gasometer to his own greenhouse.

7

Dylan and Jez were nothing if not dedicated to their work. The next morning they were up bright and early and addressing themselves to the day's tasks. This, initially, involved munching their way through part of last week's prize of Crunchy Bran Nuts (with no-cow milk) washed down with some of their lifetime's free supply of tea ('The only bag that doesn't sag!'). After that, it was time for some serious work.

By mid morning they had left the gasometer and had driven to the head office of Inventions Are Us!

Jez had discovered that this establishment, although ostensibly a private company, was actually government funded. Seventeen billion pounds had been diverted from the health and education services in order to re-establish Britain as a world-leader in inventions. Several months previously, the Prime Minister, alarmed that Britain was celebrated for its Victorian values and not much else, had set his Cabinet some unusual homework. He instructed them to make a list of all the great British inventions, with dates. There would be a lollipop for the winner.

The results confirmed the PM's worst suspicions. Most of his pupils had come up with the same answers: the telephone, the television, penicillin, trains . . . and the Sinclair C5.

'See?' said the PM. 'All of them are from last century.'

'Not,' said the Minister of Cash for Questions, sucking his lollipop, 'the Sinclair C5.'

But the PM was busy putting a red cross and a *Must try harder* beside the C5 on each of the papers. 'The C5 made us a laughing stock,' he muttered. 'We want to lead the world again. We must invent things. Alistair,' he said, turning to his right-hand man, 'can we have a Ministry of Inventions?'

'I don't think it would be in the public interest, Prime Minister.'

'We could call it something else, then. Disguise it, y'know. Pretend it doesn't exist and siphon money into it.'

The Minister of Political Perks held up a tentative hand. 'Yes, Percy?'

'How about,' suggested Percy, 'we call it the Ministry of Public Interest?'

'Brilliant!' said Alistair.

'Terrif!' said the PM. Then, with a frown, 'But where do we siphon the money from?'

That remark, of course, set off a furious row. Every Minister in the room wanted to preserve his or her patch at all costs; each of them fought like fury for their territory. Only the Minister for Domestic Violence, currently under investigation for shooting his male lover at point blank range, was unable to fight his corner.

The PM had to shout to silence the squabbling class. 'Quiet!' he yelled. 'Enough! We'll settle this in the usual way.'

The Minister of Illiteracy knew exactly what that meant. So did the Minister for the Prevention of Old People. They exchanged a despondent look. Their budgets, yet again, would be slashed.

And thus was secretly born Inventions Are Us! Much to the despair of the Prime Minister, it hadn't come up with much since its inception – but it did serve as a magnet for mad people, which pleased the Minister for the Prevention of Old People. It kept the lunatics away from his department and, consequently, kept his costs down.

Jez and Dylan looked around them at their fellow inventors in the waiting room. 'This looks bad,' said the former in doom-laden tones.

It looked not unlike a hospital waiting room – if rather more expensively decorated. Sitting under the mellow glow of the Venetian crystal chandelier was a motley collection of weirdly dressed individuals, clutching a variety of contraptions to their breasts. The man in the Chippendale chair beside the full-length Gainsborough painting was grinning maniacally at the bright red plastic object in his lap. Suddenly, and to the alarm of everyone in the room, the lid flipped open and a little head popped out.

Not to be outdone, the woman beside the Boulle cabinet

leaped up and down, shaking what looked like a giant multi-blender. The whisk fell off and rolled towards the furry object at the feet of the man lolling against the Gobelin tapestry.

Dylan turned to Jez. 'What do you mean, "This looks bad"? I don't know if you've noticed, but everything we do is "bad". Look,' he said, indicating their companions, 'there's Mother Teresa and the Brady Bunch. They're good, aren't they?' It was true: the lady with the blender did look like the famous nun, and a happy family did look like the Bradys, if a little more insane.

'Yeah,' said Jez. 'But there's Vlad the Impaler over there. And the Big Bad Wolf.'

'And us. Like I said, we're "bad". Look,' added Dylan, 'you're upset 'cos you wimped out with Georgie – and now you're losing your nerve.'

'I'm not losing my nerve. And you should never have tried to tongue Georgie. You scared her off.'

'Ha! You sit there wearing a Big Bird T-shirt, green bowling shoes and a lilac anorak, and now you tell me that *I* scared her off!'

Jez looked at his outer garment. 'It's not an anorak,' he said indignantly. 'And it's not lilac. It's *arctic pink*.'

'Oh, that's a relief! No cause for alarm, then.'

'Personal grooming,' snapped Jez, 'is your answer to everything, isn't it?'

Dylan glared at Jez for a moment. Then he smiled. 'Sorry,' he said, adjusting his tie, 'I'm just nervous. We need,' he added as he remembered why they were here, 'to stay very cool.'

Jez took a deep breath. 'We do.'

'Actually,' remembered Dylan. 'We don't.'

'What?'

'We don't need this at all.' Dylan indicated the room at large.

Jez misunderstood the gesture. He thought Dylan was pointing at something specific. 'I wasn't aware,' he said with a frown, 'that we were after a Sheraton pier glass.'

'We're not. We're not after a Sheraton pier glass, we don't have to stay cool and we don't have to be here at all.'

'Why?'

'Because,' whispered Dylan, 'when the cheques clear, we'll have two million. We don't need this.'

'So why did we come?'

'Er . . .' Dylan wasn't sure. Still, now that they *were* here . . .

'One more for the road?' he suggested.

'NO!' Jez had his eye on Mother Teresa. An electric probe had suddenly emerged from her wimple. Not good. Not at all good. 'This feels bad,' he protested. 'Let's go.'

'Yeah.' Dylan stood up. Enough was enough. 'You're right.'

Jez picked up the suitcase at his feet and followed Dylan to the door. But as they reached it, it opened from the other side and a wild-haired, goggle-eyed individual darted into the waiting room. He looked around in a manner that suggested he couldn't remember why he was here, what he was doing, or who he was. Then he looked at Dylan. 'Mr Blenheim?'

'Er . . . yes, but . . .'

The man was delighted. 'This way!' he bellowed. 'This way!'

Dylan looked at Jez. Jez looked at Dylan. Then they both

shrugged and followed the other man out of the room and into his office.

The office was in blinding contrast to the waiting room. While the former housed the knick-knacks that the Minister of Sumptuousness couldn't fit into his own house, the inner sanctum of Inventions Are Us! was starkly modern; very Philippe Starck in fact. The wild-haired man made his way over to a stainless steel desk and sat on a hideously uncomfortable looking graphite and tulipwood object that Dylan and Jez presumed was a chair. The vast desk was completely bare apart from a silicone nameplate proclaiming the goggle-eyed man as a Mr Gilzean.

'All right, lads,' he said. The beam had become a frown. Not invited to sit down (probably because there was no more furniture in the room), Jez and Dylan shuffled uncomfortably. 'Before you tell me what you've got,' continued Mr Gilzean, 'let me tell you what I'm looking for. Do you know what the Inventions Report is all about?'

'Uh . . . inventions?'

The beam returned. Mr Gilzean nodded at Dylan. 'You're catching on. See this,' he said, indicating the silicone nameplate. 'House protection is important, right?'

Dylan and Jez supposed it was but couldn't see what it had to do with a silicone nameplate.

'Right,' barked Mr Gilzean. 'Move.'

'I beg your pardon?'

Mr Gilzean indicated the suitcase. 'Show me what you've got.'

Remember the Van der Graph generator?

'Mr Gilzean,' said Dylan, adopting the tone that had so intimidated Mr Greenway and his teeth, 'let me introduce you to the future of mobile lighting. The Krypton Hand-O-

Light is a lighting device the like of which you have never seen before. Treasure this moment, Mr Gilzean, for you will retell it to your children and your children's children.'

Mr Gilzean wriggled in his chair. Through delight or discomfort Dylan couldn't be sure. Still, at least he had the man's attention. 'Today's events,' he announced in apocalyptic tones, 'will change the course of your life. Forever.' Then he turned to Jez. 'Peewit – the Krypton Hand-O-Light, please.'

Much to Mr Gilzean's consternation, Jez climbed onto the stainless steel desk, reached up to the ceiling and pulled a fluorescent light from its socket. Then, glaring at Dylan on account of the unflattering Peewit, he handed it over.

Dylan reached down to the suitcase, opened it, and extracted a tiny plastic device that served no purpose whatsoever and was, in fact, part of the innards of the seventies radio Jez had found in the skip the other day.

Mr Gilzean looked intrigued. Then Dylan clamped the tiny piece of plastic round the end of the fluorescent tube. It flickered and, like Darth Vader's rod, glowed with light.

Mr Gilzean's goggle-eyes popped even further out of their sockets. 'Good God! That's amazing! No electricity.'

Not unless you counted the Van der Graph generator in the suitcase. Dylan was holding the suitcase in one hand and the fluorescent tube in the other. And he could feel the electricity flowing through him. Yet whatever discomfort he felt was offset by Mr Gilzean's rapture.

Dylan grinned and deposited the tube on the stainless steel desk. When he removed the useless little plastic object (at the same time as he withdrew his hand – funny, that), the light went out. Mr Gilzean's face crumpled: he looked like a baby whose food had just been snatched from in front of him. Fearing that he might start to cry, Jez stepped forward. Dylan followed.

This part was trickier and involved Jez making contact with Dylan. In one casual movement, he nestled up to his friend and put a hand on his back. With the other hand he attached the plastic object to the tube and held it aloft. Again the tube lit up.

My Gilzean didn't notice that Jez appeared to be umbilically attached to Dylan, nor that Dylan seemed to be welded to his metal case. He had eyes only for the glowing tube. His mouth fell open again. 'Astonishing! Utterly astonishing!'

Dylan grinned. 'I can tell that a closer inspection is called for.'

Jez grimaced as Mr Gilzean rushed out from behind his desk. Why did Dylan always get carried away? Soon he'd be inviting the entire staff of Inventions Are Us! to try out the Hand-O-Light.

Dylan handed the briefcase to Jez. Keeping his other hand on Dylan's back, Jez moved with him towards Mr Gilzean. Then Dylan handed the excited scientist the tube and the useless object. As Mr Gilzean clipped on the latter with a trembling hand, Dylan slung an arm round his shoulder. The tube glowed once more.

Saliva began to dribble from the corners of Mr Gilzean's mouth and he began to shake. Then, to the horror of the inventors of the Krypton Hand-O-Light, he called out to his secretary. 'Jenny! Jenny! You've just got to see this.'

Jez and Dylan looked at each other as Jenny came bounding into the office. 'D'you know how to play Twister?' whispered Dylan in Jez's ear.

Jez nodded. 'It's that game where you have to contort yourself into unlikely positions.'

'Get ready.'

With Jenny they formed a cosy little foursome. Jenny put the men's proximity to each other down to excitement rather than any other inclinations. Then she dismissed all notions of those inclinations when Dylan put his arm round her shoulders. Nothing strange about that. Then she forgot about everything except her own excitement when the light in her hand went on.

Oblivious to Dylan's other arm draped on his shoulder, Mr Gilzean began to yell again. 'Marcus! Gerald! Claire! Come in here . . . this is something you just have to see!'

It was touch (literally) and go for a while, but Dylan and Jez won their game of twister. Hands down. And the other participants had experienced the greatest buzz of their lives.

Mr Gilzean wasn't just dribbling from his mouth by the time his entire staff had witnessed the wonders of the Krypton Hand-O-Light – he was pouring with sweat. He could no longer contain himself. 'Right,' he said, as his gibbering employees walked out. 'How much?'

'They're a thousand pounds each.'

Mr Gilzean looked astounded. He'd expected several thousand – and a fight about the copyright. 'Oh . . . well . . . I suppose we could afford ten – if you throw in the copyright.' Me Gilzean wasn't such a gibbering wreck that he couldn't spot a bargain when it glowed in his face. He smiled at Jez and Dylan. Poor little people, he thought. But then inventors were never great businessmen.

Sucker, thought Dylan.

Prat, thought Jez.

Then Dylan frowned. 'Well . . . there *is* a problem, actually.'

'Oh? What's that?'

Dylan hung his head in embarrassment. 'Well . . . we seem to be having a little cash flow problem at the moment. I wonder . . . I know it's a bit of a cheek, but do you think we could have a cheque today?' He turned to Jez. 'If I send Peewit here back to the factory for nine more, then you could have them later this –'

'Consider it done!' Mr Gilzean shouted to Jenny to call the Finance Director.

Peewit looked thunderous. Dylan leaned over to him. 'Here's twenty quid,' he whispered. 'That should be enough for nine tubes.'

'What about the plastic thingy?'

Dylan shrugged. 'The packaging on the tubes? Just cut 'em up and nobody'll know.'

Peewit left the room. 'I'll drop them off,' he said over his shoulder, 'in reception.'

Mr Gilzean nodded enthusiastically. 'Now, Mr Blenheim, if you'll just sign this . . . then you can pop up to Finance for your cheque.'

Mr Blenheim sighed with a flourish almost as sweeping as his smile.

Then he popped up to Finance.

James Stratton-Luce at Work

Well, that's rather given the game away, hasn't it? So much suspense could have been built up, so many pages of plot devoted to a nail-biting, climactic encounter between James Stratton-Luce and Dylan. Instead all we get is the bald fact that James happens to be the Financial Director of Inventions Are Us!

James had temporarily forgotten about Jez and Dylan (*The bastards!* as he knew them). On the day of the fabulous demonstration of the Krypton Hand-O-Light, James was sitting in his important office at Inventions Are Us!, thinking about his wife.

Eleanor had really done it this time, landed him well and truly in the soup. While James and the other residents of Cranworth Crescent had acted in a sensible, rational way and seized the Cummins's loft insulation for division amongst themselves (point three metres each), Eleanor had gone mad. Not angry mad but mad mad. So mad that James had seen no option other than to commit her to a Home for the Bewildered. He wept as he told the neighbours that it was for the best, that Eleanor was now a danger to herself (rather than him) and had to locked up, drugged, monitored for every hour of the day and generally disposed of in a humane way.

In the normal course of events this would have been entirely satisfactory. But there was nothing normal about the letter he had received that morning. It was from the Home and it stated that its budget had been slashed and that James would have to pay for the incarceration of his wife. The letter went on to explain that while release back into the community was an option for some patients, it wouldn't do in Eleanor's case. Eleanor would be a danger to society at large and 'That bastard with the small penis' in particular.

The Principal of the Home had added a postscript: *We are delighted to note that your wife has a substantial private income. This will meet most of the expenses of her stay with us. We trust that this will alleviate any financial difficulties you may have envisaged, although we are sympathetically aware that it can provide little solace to you in your grief.*

James wasn't grieving. He was apoplectic with rage. He was fizzing. Bloody Eleanor. How dare she eat up all his money being Bewildered? There was nothing for it: he would have to kill her.

So James had murder on his mind when Dylan walked into his office. But he had no intention of murdering strangers, so he looked up and smiled at the good-looking young man. Then he frowned. Hadn't he seen this person somewhere before?

Dylan showed absolutely no signs of recognition. There was not even a flicker of recall as he looked with disinterest at the nameplate on the desk. All he was interested in was his money.

'I'm sorry to rush you through this payment,' he began, 'but cash flow is always a problem . . . during expansion, you know. Ha ha.'

James knew all right. His face tightened imperceptibly yet painfully as he reached for the company chequebook. He knew exactly who this man was – and he couldn't believe his luck. There would be no more dealing with the police: James was going to take the law into his own hands. James was going to follow this man home, find out where he lived, and then retire to his own, Eleanor-less, abode to plot his revenge.

But first the cheque. James smiled at Dylan. 'That's absolutely no problem, Mr Blenheim. I've got the cheque here. I'll just sign it. There.'

James looked awfully smug as he handed over the cheque.

'Thank you,' said Dylan. 'How terribly kind.'

'Anything to oblige.'

What a polite man, thought Dylan as he left the office. Rich, too, if the suit was anything to go by. Bet he lives somewhere nice.

Georgie was smiling. The man in front of her was not. He was grimacing, his mouth bared in a sort of rictus grin that did very little to enhance his attractiveness. But Georgie wasn't interested in his face, unattractive or not. Her attention was focused on his left leg, a limb that she had just succeeded in severing from the rest of the man's body.

She stood back from the bloody mess she had created – a job, she reckoned, well done. Aware that she would have to wait for the professor's approval before she set to work on the right leg, she peeled off her surgical mask and was in the process of doing the same with her soaking gloves when she heard her name called out from the far end of the dissection room.

It was Floss. She stood in the doorway, and she looked as if she was unsure about venturing any further. Smiling a greeting, Georgie gestured for Floss to enter.

But Floss was perfectly sure about the venturing and had absolutely no intention of doing so. Georgie and her dead man were not the only people in the room: there were nine other medical students, all hacking away at various parts of different bodies. Floss remained where she was and beckoned to Georgie to come over. Then she retreated into the corridor and away from the carnage.

Georgie joined her a moment later, absent-mindedly tapping the blood-soaked gloves, garden-party fashion, against her left wrist.

Floss grimaced. 'Must you?'

'What?' Georgie looked down. 'Oh. The gloves. Sorry.'

She slipped them into her pocket, smearing the lab coat with yet more blood. Then she looked up at Floss and noticed that she was slightly flushed. 'What's up? What is it?'

'This,' said Floss, reaching into her own bloodless pocket. 'It arrived after you left.'

Georgie reached out for the telegram message. 'Oh. Wonder who it's from?' Privately, she hoped it might be from Jez, or even an apology from Dylan. But it wasn't. When she opened it she saw that it was from Roger.

Darling Georgie, it read, *the deeds are completed at last. I'm buying the foundation so the staff, the patients and your brother are all safe.* Georgie let out a delighted whoop and jumped up and down with joy. Floss, too, was over the moon. Then Georgie read the last line and stopped whooping. *My gift to you for our wedding day.*

She had, temporarily, forgotten that she was supposed to marry Roger. No such thing as a free lunch.

But the news about the foundation was great. She looked up, grinning, and handed the telegram to Floss. 'The foundation,' she explained, 'isn't going to the tax man after all.'

'I know. I rang Robin. He was ecstatic.'

'You mean,' snapped Georgie, 'you read the telegram?'

'Oh, come on . . . I'm your sister, for God's sake. Of course I read it. You read my diary . . . I borrow your knickers. Be realistic.'

But to Floss's surprise, Georgie was looking really deflated. 'Great,' she mumbled.

'What?'

'It's just that I was really looking forward to *us* doing that. You know, actually going there and letting Robin know it's all right.'

Realizing she had jumped the gun, Floss looked contrite. 'Damn. That *was* bad, wasn't it?' She reached out and squeezed her sister's arm. 'I'm sorry . . . I'm the most insensitive person in the world.'

Georgie grinned at the remark. No, she thought, that would be Dylan. 'Not quite, but I daresay you'd probably like him.' Floss was better at handling the Dylans of this world.

But Floss was still looking worried. She reached out again. 'Georgie, are you sure you're okay about this?'

Georgie forced a smile. 'Of course. Roger's lovely. He's handsome, generous . . . he's, er . . . punctual –'

'And punctuality is important.'

'Vital,' giggled Georgie.

Doubt flashed across Floss's features. 'Robin and I will be living in the house with you and Roger,' she said. 'I hope that's –'

'You'd bloody well better be,' said a vehement Georgie.

So what, exactly, is all this about? What is the foundation, who is Robin, where is the house and why will the blissfully happy young couple be sharing it? Jez and Dylan would have loved to know.

At the Races

'Go on my beauty!' yelled Roger. 'Run on!'

Several heads turned in querulous irritation to the source of the raucous roar. It really wasn't done, in the Members' Enclosure, to scream *quite* so loudly. Especially during *this* race.

'Is that,' whispered one of the heads, 'the idiot who bought old Vacuum Pack?'

'Yes,' nodded another. 'Roger Grandison. Money to burn. The very rich, as they say, are different.'

'Yes. They've got more money.'

They turned their binoculars back to the track.

Beside Roger but without binoculars, Georgie had lost sight of the horses. 'How is our Vacuum Pack doing at the moment?' she asked.

On the defensive about the horse being at the rear, Roger assumed Georgie was being sarcastic. 'He's the best horse on the field,' he snapped. Then, aware of several eyes on him again, he turned to Georgie and lowered his voice. 'It's tactical racing, darling. Every time he loses, his odds improve. If he wins the Challenge Cup his sperm will be worth two hundred thousand a throw –'

'A spurt,' corrected Georgie.

'Er . . . yes. Exactly.' Roger wasn't keen on bodily fluids. Farting, yes. Grown up stuff, no. He had, after all, been to Britain's best public school. 'And it will all be yours when we're married.'

'How romantic,' sighed Georgie. 'Horse sperm is forever.'

Roger turned his beautiful blue eyes on Georgie's beautiful brown ones. 'You just don't deserve me,' he declared.

Georgie nodded. 'You're right.'

Roger was tempted to cast caution to the wind and sweep Georgie into his arms. He knew, however, that such rashness would only result in a creased cashmere jacket and a dishevelled coiffure. Georgie might not like it either. 'God,' he said instead. 'I adore you!' Then he leaned closer and whispered, 'What are you doing for the rest of your life?'

Georgie wasn't entirely sure.

After the race (Vacuum Pack came last) they went down to the lawn to talk to Charlie Panfield. Roger called him Panties, a nickname that irritated the hell out of the jockey. Georgie knew this. Roger didn't have a clue.

'Vacuum,' said Charlie, 'is a great little ride. He just needs the right going, a little luck.'

Georgie smiled at the woebegone-looking grey. The animal looked like it would need a great deal of luck. Still, what did she know about racing?

Roger seemed to be thinking along the same lines. 'Darling,' he said in a run-off-and-play voice, 'would you mind if I just had a brief word with Panties? Y'know . . . *tactics*.'

Georgie shrugged an agreement.

As she walked away, Roger grabbed Charlie's arm. 'As soon as you get changed, pop in to see us, will you?'

'Is it about the Challenge Cup, sir?'

Roger shook his head. 'Forget the Challenge Cup, Panties.' He jabbed an angry finger at the hapless Vacuum Pack. 'That horse hasn't got enough pedigree to make it into a can of dog food. I'm going to flog the bloody nag. But . . . er, don't spread it around, there's a good chap.'

Charlie looked hurt. Roger, of course, didn't notice. 'I'll keep that just between the two of us, sir,' he said, patting the animal.

'Good egg.' Roger barrelled off in search of someone far more important; someone about whom Georgie had to remain ignorant. Which was why Roger had sent her off to play.

He found him in the champagne bar. 'Hello!' he brayed.

'Ah, Mr Grandison. Glass of champagne?'

'Splendid.'

'So,' said the other man as he poured out a glass of Bollinger, 'how's it all going?'

'Swimmingly.'

'All set for June?'

Roger nearly choked on his champagne. 'June?' he spluttered.

'Yes.' The other man's eyes narrowed. 'Is that a problem?'

'Er . . . no. Not exactly.' Help. It was a problem. A very big problem. He wasn't marrying Georgie until September.

'Because if it is a problem then we're not interested. We need it,' finished the other man, 'by the twelfth of June.'

Damn.

'Ah,' said Roger. 'You see . . . it won't be exactly mine until I'm married and . . . you see, I am not getting married until the merry month of September . . . ha ha!' he finished with a palpitating heart and a loud guffaw.

'June,' said his companion, 'is such a lovely time of year.'

'But I get terrible hay fever!'

'In which case I would say that we don't have a deal.'

But Roger needed a deal. 'Okay,' he said. 'I'll get married in June.'

'Congratulations.'

'Georgie?' He found her lurking outside the champagne tent – a little too close for comfort.

'Mmm?'

'I've been thinking.'

'Impressive.'

Roger pulled Georgie into his arms, casting caution and creased cashmere to the wind. This was an emergency. 'Oh sweetheart, let's get married sooner. June is such a lovely month.'

Georgie was appalled. 'But . . . but . . . what about your hay fever?'

'Bugger my hay fever. What do you say?'

Georgie grimaced. 'Oh. Okay.'

A marriage made in heaven.

8

This time, it really was a coincidence when Georgie bumped into Jez. She was emerging from her lawyer's office after imparting the good news. He was leaving the bank after closing the InfoTec account. Georgie was carrying a handbag. Jez was carrying a brown paper bag stuffed with fifty-pound notes.

'Jez!' Clearly delighted to see him, Georgie bounded over and pecked him on the cheek.

Jez was thoroughly confused. Their last meeting, on the roof of the gasometer, had left him with the impression that she simply wasn't interested. And now a peck.

Georgie noted his discomfiture. Then she noticed his brown bag. 'Just robbed the bank?' she teased.

Jez laughed. But he was still uneasy and Georgie knew it. 'Look,' she said in an attempt to lighten the atmosphere. 'I'm sorry about the other night on the roof . . . it's just that I wanted you to know something. You see, I'm going to get . . . I'm getting . . . that is to say . . .'

Jez laughed again. For real. 'You sound,' he said, 'like me.'

'Do I?'

'Mmm. Tongue-tied. What was it you wanted to say?'

Georgie grabbed his arm and pulled him closer. Then she giggled. 'I'm going to get a toast rack. To go with the singing toaster.'

Jez smiled at her lovely, open face. He didn't believe a word of it. Georgie had been on the verge of saying something infinitely more serious. But if that was the way she wanted to play it . . .

'Would you like to come back to my place? For a cup of tea?' The words were out before he could help himself.

'Yes,' said Georgie. 'I'd love to.'

Inside, the gasometer looked exactly the same by day as it did by night. 'Don't you ever get fed up with having no natural light?' asked Georgie.

'No.' Jez made his way to the kitchen area and switched on the kettle. 'We're very rarely here during the day anyway. We're usually . . .'

'Working?'

'Yeah. Working.' Jez had been about to say *out making money*. Still, he supposed they were one and the same thing. He walked over to the fridge. 'Would you like –?'

'No-cow milk?' Georgie was grinning from ear to ear.
'No.'

'Oh.'

'Why don't I make the tea?' Remembering the undrink-able coffee of the other day, Georgie marched over to the kettle. She nearly tripped over Jez's bag of money. 'Aren't you going to put that somewhere safe?' she asked, frowning at the crisp fifty-pound notes peering out from the top of the bag.

'Yeah. I was just about to.' Jez brushed past Georgie and, to her surprise, knelt down on the beautiful Persian rug in what Georgie supposed would have been the hallway had the gasometer had any rooms apart from the greenhouses. Then he pulled back the rug, exposing the panelled metal floor underneath.

Georgie watched, riveted, as he pulled a rusty rivet out of one of the metal plates. Beneath the rivet was a keyhole.

'What's that?' she asked.

'It's a keyhole.'

Georgie bit her lip to stop herself from giggling. 'I know that – but is it your safe or something?'

'It is indeed.' Jez fumbled inside his (non-scratch) T-shirt for the key on the chain around his neck. Then he detached it and slotted it into the hole. The whole metal panel twisted, revealing a cavity with two metal cases in it.

'What are those?' asked Georgie, as Jez lifted them out.

'The coffers.'

Georgie frowned. 'Why don't you keep it in the bank?'

'Well, 'cos we'd be helping the rich get richer and anyway, banks aren't secure.'

'Of course. Silly me.' Georgie indicated the cases again. 'So this is the two million pounds?' She didn't believe for a moment that Jez and Dylan were even halfway serious about the amount of money they hoped to raise for the orphan project.

Her sarcasm failed to register with Jez. 'Yeah,' he said absently. 'Sure is.'

'Can I see?' No one, not even Georgie, could resist the lure of oodles of crisp fifty-pound notes.

Jez looked up and shook his head. 'Sorry. I've only got the key for the safe.' He tapped one of the cases. Like its partner, it had a little red light, beating like a heart, beside the handle. 'Dylan's got the one for the cases.'

Georgie was appalled. She wouldn't entrust Dylan with a key to her cat flap. 'Do you trust him?'

Jez looked offended. 'Dylan is completely trustworthy. He's just . . . a little unreliable in some areas.' Then he caught Georgie's eye. 'I told him I thought you were unique and he tried to snog you.'

Embarrassed, Georgie looked away. 'Elegantly put, but point taken.' Oh dear, she thought, I really had better tell him about Roger.

'Jez . . .'

But then the door opened and Dylan sauntered in. He was grinning like mad and holding a large cheque in front of him. The he saw Georgie and the cases and looked immediately uncomfortable. 'Hi, Georgie,' he said without warmth. He turned to Jez. 'Why are the cases out?' The 'in front of her' was implicit in his tone.

'We can trust her,' said Jez.

Georgie smiled up at Dylan. 'You can trust me.'

But Dylan looked positively thunderous. Ignoring both of them, he stormed off to his greenhouse.

Georgie sighed, put down her newly made cup of tea

and stood up. 'Look, I'd better go . . . but Jez, I need to tell you something . . .'

Jez held up a hand to stall her. Whatever she wanted to say could wait. If it was private, as he suspected it was, he didn't want Dylan within earshot.

Nor, in point of fact, did Georgie. She picked up her bag and, with a last rueful smile, headed towards the door. 'I'll call you later,' she said. Then she left.

The minute she had closed the door behind her, Dylan shot out of his greenhouse. 'You *never*,' he growled, 'show the cases to anyone. No one.'

'I know, I know, I just –'

'No one.' In big brother mode, Dylan could be rather alarming.

Jez looked suitably chastened. 'Okay, okay. But,' he added with a child-like pout, 'I'm not a child.'

Dylan bit his lip to stop himself smiling.

Jez changed the subject. 'I picked up the cash from the InfoTec account.' Pulling a wad of fifty-pound notes out of the paper bag, he waved them, olive-branch fashion, in front of his friend.

They both knew this was more than a peace offering. This was something infinitely more momentous: the culmination of five years' arduous, relentless, back-breaking, soul-destroying (enough of that) work. It was the moment they had been waiting for since, in their respective orphanages, they had dreamed their Impossible Dreams.

Now those dreams were about to come true.

Whooping with delight, Dylan took the key to the cases from around his neck and opened them. Each was almost full of fifty-pound notes. Each was about to be completely full when the InfoTec money, split two ways, was added.

But then Dylan stood up again and, grinning wildly, rushed over to the kitchen and pounced on the soda stream. Jez looked on, baffled, as Dylan unplugged it, returned to the cases, and plugged it into a nearby socket. Then he grabbed his wad of notes, shoved it into the machine and pulled the lever. With a loud *pop!*, five thousand pounds shot into the air.

It rained money. Laughing hysterically, Jez and Dylan danced around, arms outstretched, trying to catch the money as it fluttered down towards them.

A Tender Moment

A stillness, a strange silence, descended when all the money had fallen to the ground. The two men stared at each other over the sea of notes. 'Jez,' began Dylan, taking a step forward. Then he stopped and tried to swallow the lump in his throat. 'Jez, you know . . . you know we've got no family and . . . well . . .' Dylan was finding it difficult to speak and his eyes, as he looked at Jez, were misty. He stepped closer. 'I mean, well . . . we've come a long way. You're all I've got, and . . .'

Dylan threw himself into Jez's arms. Overcome with emotion, they both felt the tears brimming as they hugged each other. 'We've done it,' whispered Jez over Dylan's shoulder. 'We've really done it.'

Both rather embarrassed after the overt display of emotion, they pulled apart and, brisk and business-like, gathered up the money and placed it in the suitcases. Then they returned the cases to the floor safe and rearranged the Persian rug over it. Still embarrassed, they cast around for something macho and laddish to do. They noticed the abandoned, half-deflated blow-up dolls nestling unhappily on the fluorescent bean bags. No, they thought. Not quite the thing. That would be sad, not macho.

And then Jez noticed the cheque that Dylan had been holding when he returned home. He picked it up from the table and looked at it. 'Er, Dylan?' he said with a frown.

'Mmm?'

'Who gave you this cheque?'

'Inventions Are Us! It's for the Krypton Hand-O-Light.'

'But who, *personally*, gave you the cheque?'

Dylan shrugged. 'The guy at accounts.'

'What was his name?'

'Umm.' Dylan's brow furrowed as he tried to remember the nameplate. 'Mr Stratton-something.'

Oh God, thought Jez. He looked again at the cheque. 'Did he have big black ears and a wiggly nose?'

'What?'

Jez handed the cheque to Dylan. 'It's signed by Mickey Mouse.'

Dylan looked down in disbelief. But it was true. There was Mickey's signature. He looked back up at Jez. 'Maybe that's his nickname?' he ventured.

Jez sighed. 'You said Stratton-something . . . could it have been Stratton-Luce?'

'Yes,' smiled Dylan, sensing a solution on the way. 'That was it.'

'Don't you remember?'

'Remember what?'

'"Mrs Stratton-Luce",' quoted Jez, imitating Dylan's dreadful Home Counties accent, '"James asked us to come round to slot in some insulation for your new abode".'

The colour drained out of Dylan's face. 'Oh my God . . . Oh my *Gawd*! Oh . . .'

But he never finished the sentence. He was interrupted by a loud banging on the door of the gasometer; a banging accompanied by the confident, plummy vowels of WPC Camilla Cash. 'Open up!' she commanded. 'Police! Dylan Zimbler and Jeremiah Quinney, you are under arrest.'

In the Dock

'Dylan Zimbler and Jeremiah Quinney,' (no messing around here – we're already at the trial) 'I have no option but to find you guilty.' Looking immensely pleased with himself, the magistrate glared at the defendants. 'Before I impose the sentence, have you anything to say?'

Dylan inclined his head and took a step forward. 'Your Honour, I'm not concerned for my own welfare, but I would like to say a few words about this man here.'

Oh God, thought Jez, what's coming now?

The magistrate nodded. 'Go ahead, but make it brief.'

Dylan took a deep breath and smiled at Jez. 'Jeremiah Quinney is the nicest, kindest, most decent person I've ever known.'

Oh, thought the court usher, how *sweet*.

'He was brought up an orphan, an outsider. No home. No family. Nowhere to run when the going got tough.'

Oh, thought the court usher, how *sad*.

Then Dylan wrapped his arms round his chest and affected what he reckoned was a Jez-like expression. 'Mummy, mummy, it's cold,' he said in a child's voice. 'Can I come in now?'

Oh for heaven's sake, thought the court usher. You've blown it now.

Reverting to his normal voice and stance, Dylan prodded Jez in the ribs. 'He's been pushed around, laughed at, humiliated. He's failed with women –'

'Dylan!'

'– and now he finds himself in a courtroom. Why?' Dylan leaned forward. 'I'll tell you why. It's because there was never anyone there to make a difference. Today, your Honour, you could make that difference.'

The magistrate slammed his gavel on the bench. 'Three months for the pair of you!'

As deflated as his dolls, Dylan sat down again.

'Well,' muttered Jez, 'that made a difference.'

But the magistrate hadn't finished. 'What,' he barked, 'are your financial circumstances?'

Well, that was easy. 'We're broke,' they said in unison.

The magistrate frowned. 'What is your profession?'

'We're entrepreneurs.'

Oh bum, thought the magistrate. They really must be broke. He knew all about entrepreneurs. What was the name of that chappie? The one who invented the disastrous C5? Poor beggar. 'I order you,' he finished, 'to repay the sum embezzled and costs at a rate of fifty pence per week.' Then he turned to the court usher. 'Next!'

But his sentence induced pandemonium in the visitors' gallery. James Stratton-Luce, his neighbours in Cranworth Crescent and Dave Ray shot to their feet. 'Outrageous!' screamed James.

'Pathetic!' cried Mrs Furnival-Jones.

'Bleedin' disgrace!' yelled Dave Ray, risking contempt of court. Then he turned to James and whispered in his ear, 'How about a little drink and a chat?'

James nodded. Dave Ray was, of course, insufferably common – but James knew that desperate measures were called for. If he combined his brains, looks, charm, cunning and style with Dave's . . . well, common thuggish touch, he was sure that justice could be done. His type of justice. A slow smile spread across his pale features as he accepted the invitation. The smile broadened as, out of the corner of his eye, he saw Jez and Dylan being marched off to prison.

9

Jez and Dylan rather enjoyed prison. It certainly beat the hell out of their respective orphanages. It was less restrictive, there were fewer bullies, the food really wasn't bad, they had an en-suite loo in their room and, to their delight, they found that hobbies were encouraged. Dylan signed up for the lock-making course; Jez spent many a happy hour in the computer class, hacking into the database of the Ministry for the Privatization of Prisons. He was appalled by the some of the information he unearthed. The catering in the Prison for Politicians, for example, was franchised out to the Ritz. And administration costs at the Open Prison for Party Donors had been halved, so it was claimed, by re-locating it to Jamaica. But Jez was most interested in the Prison for the Aristocracy: it was housed in a truly magnificent stately home.

The best thing about the prison where Jez and Dave were incarcerated was that there were no fearsome figures of authority like Miss Biggins or Miss Van der Pump. (Miss Biggins, of course, was in her own prison, having a splendid – if slightly bewildering – time with the spirited Eleanor Stratton-Luce. Miss Van der Pump was no more. Having reached the age of fifty without managing to secure herself a husband, she shut herself in her apartment, was forgotten about, and died.) In the place of these terrifying ladies were several obliging men in uniform who were delighted to help Jez and Dylan – for a small consideration – with various scams. True, there was little money to be made out of them, but they helped pass the time and kept Jez and Dylan in champagne, foie gras, decent claret, some rather fine hampers from Fortnum's and, for Dylan, endless cigarettes. All in all, it wasn't a bad way to spend three months.

There was only one real downside to prison as far as Jez was concerned: no Georgie. He pined. Dylan pined for Burt Bacharach and Barry White.

After two and a half months they were beginning to get bored. They had enrolled in more courses (although Dylan sold his place on Getting Back to Work to a resident who actually was planning a career change), they had decorated their cell in Regency stripe, they had read every book in the prison library until they had crime coming out of their ears and they had, via a subscription to *Country Life*, located the stately home they wished to buy. The several estate agents currently residing with them in prison had given them several handy hints on negotiating techniques. Now all they wanted to do was get out and buy it.

Exactly fourteen days before they were due to be released, Jez's world fell apart. He was in the midst of his morning routine, sitting on his bunk sipping his coffee and nibbling his divinely crumbly croissant, when it happened. He let out a long, low moan.

'What's up?' said Dylan, puffing on a duty free Marlboro Light in the bunk below.

'Georgie,' mumbled Jez, rustling the newspaper.

'*Georgie?*' Surely not. Georgie couldn't be moving in? He wouldn't have thought prison was her kind of place. 'She's not coming to stay, is she?'

'No. Much worse.' Jez stared, wide-eyed, at the newspaper. 'She's getting married.'

'*Married?*'

Jez looked down in annoyance. 'I find your tone rather offensive. She's a very attractive girl. It shouldn't be surprising that someone wants to marry her.'

'So why are you surprised, then?'

'I'm not. I'm just . . . well . . .'

But Dylan knew exactly how Jez felt – and felt for him. He stubbed out his cigarette in the RITZ HOTEL ashtray and clambered up to join his friend. He put a comforting arm round Jez's shoulders as he read the short article and looked at the accompanying photograph of Georgie and a prat.

'Oh God!' he exclaimed. 'Oh no. *Oh no!*'

The second *no* was nothing short of a wail. Jez was touched. He didn't know that Dylan cared so much. Maybe prison had softened him.

'No,' said Dylan again, this time in a whisper.

He's going to cry, thought Jez. Sweet.

Then he noticed that Dylan wasn't looking at the Georgie page but at the business section opposite. Pride of place was given to a large photograph of a fifty-pound note. Below the photograph was the headline that Dylan was still looking at in horror. It read FIFTY-POUND NOTE TO BE WITHDRAWN.

No, thought Jez. This is not possible. This cannot happen.

But it could.

An emergency measure by the Bank of England, ran the paragraph below, *will mean that the fifty-pound note will cease to be legal tender after the thirtieth of June, thirteen hundred hours GMT. The Palace won its High Court claim that the Queen's likeness is unflattering and therefore defamatory.*

Jez went whiter than the Egyptian cotton sheets on his bunk. 'The thirtieth of June,' he whispered. 'That's one day before we're released . . .'

Dylan began to cry. 'We're going to be the proud possessors of two million quid of useless notes – and all because the Queen doesn't like her picture. Jesus Christ!' he shouted as anger took over. 'It's self, self, self with some people!' Then he jumped off the bunk and began to pace the cell. 'There's got to be a way round this. There's got to be. I haven't waited eighteen years to be robbed blind by a pensioner – Queen or no Queen.'

On the bunk, coffee and croissant forgotten, Jez was still looking ashen. Then he found his voice. 'But surely we can change the money – after that date.'

Dylan whirled round. 'Sure – but aren't they going to have some questions to ask if we take two million quid in fifty-pound notes to a bank? Talk to the police, maybe?'

'Oh.' Dylan was right – and Jez didn't fancy another interrogation by the frightening Camilla Cash. 'What about buying something expensive?' he suggested.

'Yes, that's the one good thing about prison, isn't it? The shopping facilities really are excellent. We play our cards right and we could end up with two million pounds worth of tobacco and Pamela Anderson posters.'

'But the black market . . . ?'

'Oh get real, Jez. We'll end up with knives in our throats if we let on about how much money we've got. Beluga caviar –'

'It's Sevruga, actually.'

Dylan waved a dismissive hand. 'Caviar is one thing in prison. Two million bucks is quite another.'

'Okay, supposing we get someone to spend it for us?'

Dylan very nearly punched the wall in exasperation. 'Oh, great idea. Nick the Fence is out next week. Why don't we ask HIM TO DO IT?'

'No need to shout.'

'I'm not shouting! I'm thinking!' Dylan continued to pace. Silence fell in the small cell.

Perhaps it was the little rhyme in the above sentence that took Jez's mind back to InfoTec, to the ditty about the little teapot . . . and therefore back to Georgie.

'Georgie,' he said to himself.

'What?'

'Georgie.'

'Oh, not her again.' Dylan resumed his pacing.

'No, I meant why don't we get *her* to spend it for us?'

Dylan stopped midpace. Georgie. Well . . . she did have her merits. In fact, the more he thought about it, the more the idea appealed to him. He had heard the words *You can trust me* from Georgie's own mouth (mind you, he'd also heard them from Nick the Fence). But, unlike Nick, Georgie already knew all about the coffers under the floor of the gasometer.

And there was another reason why Georgie was the perfect candidate. She was their only friend.

Dylan turned round and grinned at Jez. 'Georgie,' he repeated. 'I like it.'

'Considering the alternatives . . .'

'What alternatives?'

'There aren't any,' said Jez.

'Exactly. So Georgie it is.'

Then they fell silent as the fundamental flaw of their plan hit them. Georgie might not like the idea.

It was Jez who articulated this possibility.

Dylan mulled over that one for a moment. 'She might like it a bit if you put it to her in person.' Then he felt for the key around his neck. 'Anyway, you'll have to. You'll have to get her to come here first.'

'And how exactly am I going to do that?'

'By writing to her and asking her to come and visit.'

Jez didn't like that idea at all. 'But I don't want her to know I'm in prison! I want her to think I'm . . .'

'Honest?'

Jez glared at Dylan. 'Decent,' he said at length.

'Then write to her.'

Jez thought about it for a moment. The more he thought about it, the more he liked the idea. After all, they had nothing to lose. Except, of course, two million pounds.

A fellow resident called Charlie the Chubb popped his

head round the door. 'Search!' he barked before hurrying off to the next cell.

'Oh, God.' This from Jez as he looked at the chain round his neck.

Dylan detached his key from his own chain. 'No choice,' he said.

Jez looked truly miserable. Apart from pining after Georgie, this was the one thing he really disliked about prison – the searches. And there was very little that could be done about them. Once a week, they and their cells were searched by the uniformed men from the dreaded H Block, or Horrid Block as it was known. These men were not open to small considerations or buckets of beluga. They meant business.

Jez sighed and detached his own key. '*Please*, Dylan,' he pleaded.

Dylan smiled in encouragement and dangled his key in front of his mouth. 'Yum, yum,' he said. Then he swallowed it.

Jez groaned.

'Tangy and hollow,' chanted Dylan. 'And easy to swallow.'

Jez swallowed.

A week later Georgie received Jez's letter. It was short and to the point, begging her to come and visit him on, appropriately enough, visiting day. But visiting day was the very day that Georgie received the letter. Problem number one.

Problem number two was that visiting day was also Georgie's wedding day.

At eleven o'clock in the morning she was ready. She stood in front of her bedroom mirror and surveyed the image in front of her. The dress, she had to admit, was beautiful. Roger had chosen it – as indeed he had organized and chosen everything else about the wedding. 'Darling,' he had said, 'I don't want you to worry your pretty little head about anything. Relax. I'll take care of all the arrangements.'

Which meant that Roger was terrified of Georgie making a cockup and letting him down in front of his Very Important Friends.

But Georgie couldn't summon a smile for the image in the mirror. It wasn't really her.

The door opened and a young man with Down's syndrome walked in. Clad in a morning suit, he was looking both happy and apprehensive.

Although unable to smile at herself, Georgie had no such problems as far as her brother was concerned. 'I'm so proud,' she beamed, 'that you're doing this, Robin.'

Robin. At last.

Robin, the Foundation, and the House

Georgie has been keeping too much to herself for far too long. No wonder she looks tired. If a problem shared is a problem halved, this bit of plot might eliminate fifty per cent of Georgie's worries. But not, sadly, for long. (There's a nasty surprise coming up shortly.)

Georgie's problem stems from the death of her father the previous year. Death duties on his estate were enormous and Georgie, Floss and Robin, orphans now, had no option but to let their sumptuous, if decaying, family home fall into the hands of the receivers. They could have handled that. What they couldn't handle was the fact that one wing of the house had been given over – by their father – to a foundation for children with Down's syndrome and that if they were to lose the house then the foundation would have to close. Not a happy scenario – especially for Robin.

Georgie and Floss's attempts to raise money to save the house, though admirable, had proved feeble. They needed an awful lot of money.

Enter Roger: rich, kind, handsome, generous, punctual Roger. If Georgie agrees to marry Roger, her share of the house and foundation will also be his. As part owner, he could pay off the receivers and then he and Georgie, Floss and Robin would live in the house and the foundation would continue. Everyone will have found their Happily Ever After.

But remember the day Roger consigned Vacuum Pack to a tin of dog food? Remember the man in the champagne tent? Remember that Roger is a prat – and not a very nice one at that?

'Dad for a day,' said Robin, back in Georgie's bedroom. 'Nervous?' he asked his sister.

'God, no,' she replied.

'No butterflies?'

'No. I feel amazingly calm.'

Robin grinned. 'It must be great to feel so sure about something.'

Georgie's heart lurched. If only you knew, she thought. If only you knew. But he didn't know; Georgie had sworn never to reveal to him her true feelings about Roger. 'Yes,' she said. 'It is.' Then, forcing a smile, 'You know, I thought I'd be a nervous wreck, but I feel really great.'

'That's good.' Robin grinned again. 'I'm terrified.' Then he turned and left the room.

Floss bounded in a moment later. Dressed simply but elegantly in cream taffeta, she looked almost as ravishing as her sister.

She was also looking flushed. And she was carrying a letter.

'That for me?'

'Yes,' said Floss.

'Have you already read it?'

'Are you wearing my knickers?'

They laughed. The answer was 'yes' and 'yes'.

Georgie looked at the unfamiliar handwriting. 'Who's it from?'

'Jez.'

Georgie's heart missed a beat. 'Where is he? He just disappeared.'

'In prison.'

'PRISON?' Another missed beat. 'Oh my God. Why?'

Floss shrugged. 'He doesn't say. All he says is that –'

'Oh my God! He wants me to see him today?' Georgie stared, open-mouthed, at the missive.

'Yes.'

'But what do I do?' Georgie looked helplessly at her wedding dress. Not, she reckoned, standard prison visiting kit.

Floss reached out and held her by the shoulders. 'Georgie. You can't go. You know you can't go. You're getting married.'

'But –'

'I'll be there with you. It's the right thing to do, Georgie.'

It wasn't.

An hour later, Roger's Rolls rolled up outside the grand country church that Roger had chosen for the wedding ceremony. Roger's uniformed chauffeur was driving. Georgie and Floss were in the back seat. The blushing bride looked the very picture of abject misery. The bridesmaid wasn't oozing pizzazz either. The chauffeur, on the other hand, looked smugly content.

The car was very late. Like everything else about the wedding, this had been orchestrated by Roger. What was normally seen as a bride's prerogative was, on this occasion, a deliberate move on Roger's part. The longer Georgie was delayed, the more time he would have to talk to his Very Important Friends. Georgie's friends didn't count: they were massively unimportant and, anyway, desperately thin on the ground. The groom's side of the aisle was bursting, the bride's nearly empty. Georgie and Floss's old nanny had managed to escape from the Home for the Bewildered (and the dreadful Miss Biggins and her new friend – a Sharon if ever there was one) for the day while two old school friends of Georgie's had managed, despite Roger's stone-walling, to find out the date of her nuptials. That was it as far as the bride's side went – apart from Robin. Roger had tried every trick in the book to ban Robin from the wedding, but Georgie had been adamant. No Robin, no wedding. Mindful of his reasons for marrying, Roger had been obliged to capitulate. The wedding had to go ahead at all costs.

Roger's chauffeur knew this, yet he had decided he would be damned if he was going to help Georgie out of the car. Let her stew, he thought. (The chauffeur had his reasons for resenting Georgie, but this is a family saga so we'll brush swiftly past them.)

Georgie couldn't have cared less whether or not the ghastly man opened her door. As far as she was concerned, the sooner the whole gruesome process was over the better.

She already had one hand on the door handle when Roger's carphone rang.

'I'll answer it,' said Floss. 'You go and see how Robin's doing.'

'Okay. See you at the door, then.' Georgie gathered up the folds of her dress, opened the door and dashed off into the church. Most un-bride-like. But this was a very un-wedding-like wedding.

It was also a very peculiar phone call. The chauffeur wasn't aware that the phone had rung until Floss was well into a conversation that would change the plot forever.

So listen carefully.

'Hello?' said Floss, as she picked up the receiver. The line was appalling. At first there was only a crackle at the other end. Then a voice vaguely familiar to Floss started bellowing down the line. 'There you are! I've been trying your bloody mobile for the last hour. Listen . . . it's sorted. I've secured the eviction order for the closing of the foundation. The deal will go through in time for your clients.'

Floss's eyes nearly popped out of her head.

'As soon as you've signed the register,' finished the plot-changing voice, 'let me know.'

'Who is this?' demanded Floss.

'Roger?' said the voice. *Oh Christ*, the caller thought, *I've been talking to the wrong person.*

'Who,' repeated Floss, 'am I talking to?'

Mr Nobody. The line went dead.

The chauffeur turned round and saw the phone in Floss's hand. Miss Floss (how he hated that name) was not supposed to answer Mr Roger's phone. Mr Roger's phone was strictly private. He leaped out of the driver's seat and, before Floss knew it, had wrested the phone from her.

'Hey!' she yelled.

The chauffeur joined her in the back seat. 'You shouldn't,' he leered, 'have answered that.'

'Don't be ridiculous. I'm perfectly capable of answering a phone.' Floss held her head up high. 'I'm a receptionist by night, you know.'

'And what are you by day?'

Floss grimaced at the chauffeur. Apart from the fact that he was revolting looking (and jolly rude), he had a personal hygiene problem. Floss lunged for the door. 'By day,' she said, 'I'm a bridesmaid.'

'Oh no you're not.' The chauffeur reached out to stop her.

'Oh yes I am!'

'Oh no you're not.' The chauffeur locked her door.

'Oh yes I am!' Floss threw herself against it.

The chauffeur locked the entire car by remote control. 'Oh no you're not!' he crowed.

Floss was beginning to get desperate. 'Look,' she said. 'This is ridiculous. Georgie'll notice I'm not there.'

A fair assumption, given that Floss was the only bridesmaid.

'I don't care what Georgie notices,' replied the chauffeur, forgetting the 'Miss'.

Floss did some quick thinking. 'I say! Have you ever . . . well, have you ever done "it" in a Rolls-Royce?'

The chauffeur looked terrified. He had indeed done "it" in a Rolls-Royce – and what damn good fun it had been. But he didn't fancy doing "it" in Mr Roger's car with Miss Floss. The very idea –

'Or,' said Floss, waving a red rag in front of a bull, 'are you too scared?'

'Scared?' The chauffeur looked petrified.

'Yes. Scared. Or do you have other . . . ?'

'Other what?'

Floss was just about to ask the chauffeur if, perhaps, he harboured 'other' inclinations when he lunged at her.

'No!' he screamed. 'I am most certainly not terrified. Nor do I have "other" inclinations,' he lied. 'I know exactly what I'm doing!'

So did Floss. She kneed him in the groin. Then she reached for the carphone.

Georgie was livid with her sister. What was she doing wittering on the phone when she should have been providing moral support to her nearest, dearest, and almost departed? If Floss had been here she would have been able to prevent poor nervous Robin from whisking her down the aisle with such alacrity and depositing her, with Roger, by the altar. It was all rather horrid.

And now the priest was rabbiting on about having and holding. In fact, he had nearly finished rabbiting on about having and holding.

'. . . in sickness and in health,' the cleric intoned, 'to love and to cherish, till death do you part?'

'I do,' said Roger.

The vicar nodded and turned to Georgie. 'Do you, Georgina Elizabeth Victoria, take Roger Edward Neville to be your legally wedded husband, to have and to hold from this day forward, for better for worse, for richer for poorer, in sickness and in health, to love and to cherish, till death do you part?'

Georgie took a deep breath. 'I –'

Suddenly, a high-pitched bleeping sound echoed through the church, stalling Georgie in her tracks and causing consternation amongst the entire congregation. Because the majority of them were Very Important People they were armed to the hilt with mobile phones, pagers and electronic bleepers. And the problem, in this confined, echoing space, was that no one was quite sure who was being phoned, paged or bleeped. Suddenly the ceremony was forgotten as handbags were opened, breast pockets investigated and wrists examined.

At the altar, Georgie looked at Roger. Roger looked at Georgie. Then they both looked at the vicar. He squirmed. Then he lifted his cassock, pulled out his mobile and turned it off.

The ringing, however, continued.

The three of them turned to face the congregation. High fashion had given way to high technology; Max Mara and morning suits had fallen by the wayside of the microchip. The place was awash with mobiles and pagers. But still the ringing continued.

It dawned belatedly on Roger that he could well be the culprit. As furtively as he could, he reached into his breast pocket and extracted his mobile. It was bleeping away like mad.

Roger turned away from Georgie and the priest. Wedding or no wedding, he still had a large and Very Important business empire to run. 'Hello?' he whispered into the mouthpiece. 'Yes?'

Georgie raised her eyebrows. Typical. Absolutely typical.

But it turned out to be absolutely atypical. Roger recoiled in horror and handed the phone to his betrothed. 'It's for you,' he said, bristling with disapproval.

'Oh.' Now who would be calling her at this hour? 'Hello?' It was Floss.

Georgie was glad she was wearing a veil: it muffled the

sound of their conversation and, she hoped, disguised her expression. For her eyes opened wider with every syllable uttered by Floss. 'He's been lying to you!' whispered the latter. 'It's all a con. He wants to get his hands on the house and then flog it. He's already got a buyer lined up.'

'Ah,' said Georgie.

'Don't marry him!'

'Okay.' Georgie switched off the phone and handed it back to Roger. She felt an immense calm descend on her. Sorrowful rather than angry, she looked into Roger's eyes. Yes, she thought to herself. He has no soul. I always suspected it. Now I know it.

She turned to the vicar with a sad smile. 'Before I say this, let me just tell you that I really am terribly, terribly sorry.'

Then she turned back to Roger. 'You SHIT!' she spat.

The Very Important Friends looked on in utter amazement as Georgie threw him one last, vicious look and then ran past them down the aisle.

On the bride's side of the church, Nanny leaned over to Georgie's friends. 'I think I prefer the more traditional sort of service,' she declared. 'Rather more dignified.' She turned to look at Georgie flying down the aisle. 'No,' she said to herself, 'I really *don't* like running brides.'

Nor did Roger. He was aghast. He couldn't believe it, simply couldn't believe it. Georgie had made him look a fool in front of his friends.

10

'She's not coming.'

'She'll be here.'

'You reckon?'

'Yeah. So what if she's late? It's a girl's prerogative. Anyway, it's just as well she's not here yet.' Jez cast a meaningful look at Dylan. 'You haven't been, have you?'

Dylan looked sheepish. 'Um . . . no.' He patted his abdomen. 'But I think activity is imminent.'

The bully boys from Horrid Block had paid them another visit the previous day, obliging them to participate in yet another bout of key-swallowing. While Jez had difficulty with that part of the procedure, he had no problems in the key-retrieval department (Nanny would have called him 'regular'). But Dylan was very irregular.

He slunk off to the loo.

Ten minutes later he was back.

Jez looked up enquiringly.

Dylan shook his head.

Nanny would have rung for prunes.

But there were no prunes in the visitors' room. Nor was there any Georgie. But Jez was still hopeful. He was also mulling over a change of plan. 'You know we told Georgie we're Robin Hoods of the nineties?'

'Yeah.'

'Well . . . how would you feel if she found out the truth?'

Dylan was appalled. 'The bottom would fall out of my world.' He patted his abdomen again. 'On the other hand, the world might fall out of my bottom.'

'Don't be so revolting.'

'Well, don't even think about telling Georgie the truth. You're cracking, Jez.'

Jez glowered at his friend. 'I am not cracking. I'm just thinking that maybe Georgie wouldn't . . .'

But whatever Georgie wouldn't do or think was overshadowed by what Georgie actually did. As Jez spoke, the door at the end of the visitors' room burst open, revealing a breathless Georgie and a somewhat crumpled wedding dress.

Jez was gobsmacked. Dylan was astonished. They stared open-mouthed as the gorgeous apparition came floating towards them.

Georgie grinned shyly and sat down in the chair opposite Jez.

'You came.'

Georgie shrugged. 'Well, I was just passing and –'

'You're married?' A reasonable question, under the circumstances.

Georgie shook her head. 'No, I'm not.'

Jez clenched his fist under the table. Yes! Or maybe no. Maybe she had just popped in on her way to the altar. He unclenched the fist and leaned forward. 'But . . . ?'

'The wedding's off.' Georgie took a deep breath, wondering whether to burden Jez with her troubles. No, she thought, he had enough of his own. 'I've decided,' she said instead, 'to be honest with myself. If I do that then maybe others will be honest with me.'

Jez looked guilty. Dylan slunk away with an embarrassed ''scuse me.'

'Where's he going?' asked Georgie.

'Loo.'

'Oh.' Georgie leaned across the table. 'So. You asked me to come. What can I do for you?'

Jez took a deep breath. With Dylan out of the room . . .

'Georgie.' Jez leaned forward as well. 'I want to be honest with you.'

Georgie smiled. Oh goody. Then she noticed how pained he was looking. 'Jez? What's wrong?'

Another deep breath. 'Well, the money we've saved . . .'

Georgie nodded. 'You were dishonest getting it. That's all right.'

Jez couldn't quite meet Georgie's eye. 'Yes . . . but . . . yes . . .'

'You did it for a good cause. And you took it from people who could afford it.' After the wedding fiasco, Georgie was feeling particularly vindictive towards rich people. And Important People. 'Look,' she added, 'if you're worried about the money while you're . . . while you're in here, I could give it direct to your orphan project.'

Jez had never felt so wretched in his life. 'Well . . . you could, but you see . . . you see, the orphan project is . . . well . . .'

Dylan came running back into the room in the nick of time. 'It would affect the tiny government handout they're getting this year,' he said in desperation. Then he turned to Jez. 'And there's another small problem.' He pointed to his nether regions.

Jez groaned. 'The key?' he whispered.

'Yeah. It's like rush hour in there. Gridlock.'

Georgie looked on in confusion. What on earth were they on about?

Jez told her. Or at least he told her as much as he could without being dishonest. Which wasn't very much. 'We want to give you the money for safekeeping but . . . well . . . the key to the cases is . . .'

'Temporarily unavailable.'

'Yes. Thank you, Dylan.' Jez leaned forward again and handed his key to Georgie. 'This is the key to the floor-safe.'

'Oh yes. I remember.'

'Would you . . . would you go to the gasometer and get the cases?'

'Sure.'

'Will you keep them with you?'

Georgie grinned. 'Are you joking? Of course I'll keep them with me. It's not every day a girl gets given two million pounds.'

Dylan frowned. Supposing Georgie had ideas about scampering off on a spending spree? He wouldn't entirely blame her. 'They've got an explosive security system,' he said hurriedly. 'If . . .'

Georgie looked put out. 'Dylan. Dylan. I'm not going to open them. I hoped you'd know me better then that.' Then she stood up. 'Jez?'

'Mmm?' Jez turned his soulful eyes on the bride.

Georgie reached out to touch his arm. 'You're a bit special, aren't you?'

Jez went bright pink. Georgie went back to London. Dylan went to the loo.

'I'm special,' repeated Jez for the umpteenth time. 'I'm special. Special.' He sauntered down the corridor, as if floating on air.

'Oh, for heaven's sake.' Beside him, Dylan was beginning to get extremely irritated. And jealous. Nobody had ever told him he was special.

'I'm special.'

'Quiet! I'm trying to think.'

A dreamy smile on his face, Jez took to reciting the word in his head.

'Right.' Dylan had evidently thought. 'We've got to get out. It's the only way to get the money. We get ourselves hospitalized.'

'Spe – sorry?'

'We get taken to the nearest hospital and we escape from there.'

'Escape?'

'Yes. We can't escape from here. It's a prison.'

'True – but how do we get ourselves to hospital?'

Eyes shining, Dylan turned to Jez. 'Hit me.'

'What?'

'Hit me.'

'Why?'

'Because if we rough each other up we'll get taken to hospital.'

'Oh. All right, then.' Jez pushed Dylan gently against the wall.

'No. Harder!'

Jez patted his friend's stomach.

'Oh, for heaven's sake! I'll hit you then.' Dylan adopted a fierce expression and worked himself up to a violent frenzy. Then he poked Jez in the ribs.

It was hopeless. Neither of them could bring themselves to hit the other.

'Okay.' Dylan thought again. 'I know! We attack someone and get him to beat us up.'

'Sounds good.'

In the gantry on their way back to their cell, they cast around for a suitable assailant. As luck would have it, a six-foot-six bodybuilder with a bull neck and bulging biceps came loping towards them.

They exchanged a look. Then, as one, they launched themselves on the unsuspecting giant.

To no avail. They bounced off him and fell to the ground. The bodybuilder leaned down and, to complete their humiliation, picked them up again. 'Are you two all right?' he asked in a soft, gentle voice. 'You really ought to be more careful.'

Winded and not a little ashamed, Dylan and Jez could only nod. The giant patted them both on the shoulder, all but sending them spinning to the ground again. 'Take care,' he said and went on his way.

'Right,' said Dylan when he had regained his breath.

'Desperate measures call for desperate actions . . . or something.' He looked over the metal balustrade of the gantry. The gentle giant had ambled down the stairs and was now almost directly beneath them. Dylan looked at Jez. 'You ready?'

Jez nodded. Then, Dylan beside him, he vaulted over the balustrade.

At least their aim was true. They landed directly on top of the gentle giant. He roared with laughter as, again, they bounced off him and fell to the ground. Still laughing, he leaned down to help them up again. 'You two really crack me up,' he said. 'You really do.'

But the prison guards didn't share his amusement. The two who were witness to Jez and Dylan's antics had recently been chastised by the governor for being too lenient. Here was their chance to make amends. Here was their chance to show how tough they were – and, hopefully, to make a little money on the side. One never knew how much Jez and Dylan might be prepared to pay for a spot of leniency.

But – give or take the odd two million pounds – Jez and Dylan were flat broke. The guards hauled them off to the maximum security wing.

Georgie Learns the Gruesome Truth

'We *have* to get that money changed.' Dylan paced the small cell. No Regency stripe here – the only decorations were tobacco stains and a tattered Pamela Anderson poster. But interior design was the last thing on either of their minds.

'Have some more prunes,' urged Jez. He counted the

stones from those already eaten. 'Tinker, tailor, soldier, sailor. Rich man, poor man, beggar man . . . ha ha . . . thief! How appropriate.'

'Oh, shut up,' snapped Dylan. 'This is serious.'

'So is your bowel problem. Baked beans?' he offered, gesturing to the half-empty plate. 'I mean it, Dylan. We can't do anything more until we get the key.'

'Yes, we can. We can plan.'

'Oh, yeah? Like we planned to get taken to hospital?'

Dylan picked up a prune and popped it into his mouth. 'We shouldn't have picked on a weakling.'

Jez rolled his eyes.

'We have to get Georgie back here,' said Dylan.

'Only if we have the key.'

'We'll have the key. We'll have the key.' As he spoke, Dylan's stomach rumbled. The prunes and the baked beans were doing their stuff.

Five minutes later, so did Dylan.

They phoned Georgie that evening and, because visiting day in the maximum security wing happened to be the following day (convenient, that), she reappeared barely twenty-four hours after her last visit. She looked like a different person – no wedding dress and no make-up – and Jez thought she looked even more gorgeous. He was deeply, madly in love.

Dylan was just mad. He couldn't believe his eyes as the guard ushered them into the interview room. No big open space like the one they had been in the day before. This was a poky cubicle. On the other side of the glass partition was another poky cubicle in which sat the smiling Georgie.

It was the partition that sent Dylan into a frenzy. He looked at it in open-mouthed horror. It was solid plateglass.

It couldn't, simply *couldn't*, be true. 'What's this?' he wailed. 'What's this?' Then he banged his head against the glass. 'Oh, for crying out loud! They always have a little gap. *Always . . .'*

There was no gap; no way they could pass the key to Georgie. The key that Dylan himself had passed with such difficulty would remain with him. He began to cry.

Seemingly unaware of the problem, Jez was still staring goofily through the glass. Heart a-flutter, he picked up the communications phone on his side.

'Hi, Georgie.'

Without taking her eyes off him, she too picked up her phone. 'Hi.'

Then Dylan grabbed Jez's phone. 'Georgie,' he wailed, 'you've gotta help us.' He covered the mouthpiece and turned to Jez. 'Tell her how to disarm the cases.'

Jez shook his head. 'Not possible. She needs the key.'

'What about a saw?'

'Too risky.' And the last thing Jez wanted was to expose Georgie to risk. (He had handily forgotten that they were in a maximum security jail discussing two million pounds of ill-gotten gains.)

Dylan took his hand off the mouthpiece. 'I'm a broken man,' he sobbed. 'You've got to help me, Georgie.'

Georgie looked distinctly unimpressed.

'Us,' added Dylan hastily. He put an arm round Jez's shoulders. 'You've got to help us, Georgie.'

Georgie shrugged. 'Okay. I'll try.'

Still in a frightful state, Dylan nodded absently and opened the door of the cubicle. 'I need to be alone,' he mumbled. 'With my thoughts.'

Eat your heart out, Greta Garbo.

Jez was still staring at Georgie, but the goofy expression had given way to one of resolution. He was going to come clean.

'Look, Georgie,' he began, 'the money in the cases . . . the money . . .' Then he faltered, struck dumb by the weight of his imminent confession.

On the other side of the partition, Georgie nodded her encouragement.

'The poor people . . .'

'What?'

'The poor people . . .'

'Yes?' Oh for heaven's sake, thought Georgie. It can't be that bad.

It wasn't. It was infinitely worse.

'We . . . well . . . *we're* the poor people.'

At first Georgie didn't react. Reluctant to decipher the meaning of the words, her brain lagged behind her hearing. Then it clicked into gear and Georgie's mouth fell open. 'You mean,' she stammered, 'you kept all the money for yourselves. You *lied* to me?'

Jez bowed his head. 'We're orphans,' he said in a child-like whimper. 'We've never had a home.'

Georgie's world was falling apart. First Roger had let her down – but at least she'd always known he was a prat. And at least Roger had been, on the surface, 'her sort'. Jez was a different kettle of fish altogether. Her feelings for him had been much more complicated. Part of her – the part that squirmed at the very mention of anorak-wearing, badly coiffed scientific toaster fanatics – had simply refused to believe that she could fall in love with him. Another part of her had nimbly hurdled over those obstacles, urging her onto a finishing post called Happily Ever After.

So the anorak-objecting part had been right after all. Jez was a prat. He was a cheap crook. And he had been lying to her all along. Men.

Georgie glared long and hard at the cringing criminal on the other side of the partition. Then she stood up and, without a backward glance, left the cubicle.

Dylan was apoplectic with rage. 'I cannot believe,' he screamed as he paced, 'that you told her! I just cannot believe it!'

Jez hung his head. His world was in ruins. He knew hatred when he saw it – and that emotion had blazed from Georgie's beautiful eyes. Never again would her luscious lips pout round the word *special*.

'You're a schmuck, a loser,' snapped Dylan. 'What do you think she's going to do now? She's poor, she's got our cases and she's been dicked. We'll never see her again.'

What Georgie Did Next

Dylan was wrong about never seeing Georgie again. He didn't credit her with the brains, ingenuity, resolution and powers of recovery she undoubtedly possessed. He didn't know that Nanny had instilled into her the importance of *jolly well getting on with it*.

And he didn't know that the tables had turned. He wasn't aware that Georgie was developing a Grand Plan that involved using him and Jez more than they had ever used her.

Georgie went to the gasometer to retrieve the cases. (We

know how she would do this so we'll steam ahead to the place marked MORE PLOT.)

Georgie went to see her Mr Collyns, her lawyer.

Mr Collyns was a worm and, appropriately, he squirmed when she marched into his office. He hadn't expected to see her again. He knew that her world had fallen apart, that she had called off the wedding, that she was of no further use to him. Apart from the small (large, actually) matter of his fees, Georgie was history.

Or so he had thought. Now here she was, looking horribly confident and pestering him about the eviction orders and her silly foundation. It was too, too squirm-making.

For her part, Georgie was getting annoyed with Mr Collyns. Evasive was the word that sprang to mind every time she asked a question.

She tried again. 'If Roger had got the eviction orders, where would he have got them from?'

Beside her on the sofa, Mr Collyns squirmed and refused to meet her eye. 'Oh . . . any lawyer.'

'That's helpful.'

Mr Collyns shrugged.

Georgie took a deep breath. 'If I want to save our house, the foundation and the grounds, what do I need?'

'It's getting a little late for that.'

'How much?' persisted Georgie.

Mr Collyns smirked. 'One and a half million pounds.'

To his surprise, Georgie didn't bat an eyelid.

'But with duties and my fees,' he continued, 'about two million.'

'By when?'

'Next week.'

Georgie's expression remained completely inscrutable.

Then, without another word, she stood up and left the sumptuous office.

Mr Collyns's eyes narrowed. There was something going on here, he surmised. Something fishy. And Mr Collyns knew all about fishiness. Stringing Georgie along had been like shooting fish.

But now Georgie was up to something. Mr Collyns didn't like that at all. As soon as the door closed behind her, he reached for the phone.

Georgie went straight from Mr Collyns's office to the medical school. Dylan would have been horrified so see her heading for the medical stores and borrowing, for her own purposes, a large rotary saw.

But those purposes were not the ones Dylan feared. He would have breathed a sigh of relief to see her heading for the dissection room and hacking the legs off an elderly male corpse. And he would have been intrigued and not a little puzzled to see what she did with the corpse and the legs.

Then Georgie went home and made several phone calls.

Her final act of the day was to go out and buy a veil.

11

The Death of the Fifty-pound Note

'You're both wanted in the governor's office.'

Slumped in terminal gloom, Dylan and Jez barely registered that the guard had entered their cell.

'We're what?' said Dylan after a short silence.

'You're wanted in the governor's office.' The guard, they both noticed, was wearing an oddly embarrassed expression.

'Oh.' They stood up. Neither of them were particularly interested in why they were wanted. Neither of them cared. The light had gone out of their lives. They were back where they had been eighteen years ago: two impoverished orphans in an institution.

The guard ushered them out and down several corridors towards the governor's office. Then, in a strangely reverential manner, he opened the door, bowed slightly, and gestured for them to enter.

Neither Dylan nor Jez had been invited into the room before and, as they walked over the threshold, they were plunged deeper into depression. The place was furnished like the reading room of a gentleman's club: all chesterfields and bookcases. It reminded them of the library in one of the stately homes they had perused in the pages of *Country Life*.

Then they noticed that the governor, a Mr Dickens, was not alone in the room. There was a lady standing opposite him and she was clad from head to toe in black. Hearing them enter, she turned to face them. Her own face was practically invisible. A black veil was draped over her head and, underneath it, she was wearing sunglasses.

Jez had always reckoned that Georgie would look beautiful even in a binliner. Now, to his intense surprise, here she was, clad in the closest she would ever come to that particular ensemble, and she looked stunning. (Given that her entire outfit was by Chanel, she damned well should have.)

Like Jez, Dylan could only stare at the wondrous apparition in front of them. Mr Dickens, presented with a splendid view of Georgie's pert posterior, did his fair share of staring as well.

Then Georgie lifted the veil, put one black-gloved hand to her face and dabbed at her nose with a black lace handkerchief.

'Jeremiah,' she said. 'Dylan.' Then, voice quavering, she imparted her dreadful news. 'Lesley has died.'

A profound silence filled the room. Jez hadn't quite taken the information on board and was still staring at Georgie, a kaleidoscope of conflicting emotions clamouring in his head.

It was Dylan who broke the silence. A little quicker off the mark than his friend, he suddenly put one horrified hand to his mouth. 'Lesley?' he intoned. 'Not ... Lesley?'

Georgie nodded.

'Oh no! Oh nooooo . . .' Dylan seemed to shrink visibly before them. His shoulders slumped, his knees all but gave way and he began to rock back and forth on his heels (all tricks he'd learned from the deflating dolls). Then he burst into tears.

Jez was completely mystified. 'Who's dead?'

'Lesley,' snapped Georgie, willing him to click. 'Lesley's dead.'

But Jez was even more puzzled. 'Who's Lesley?'

'Our Lesley,' moaned Dylan. 'Dead? It can't be true. So young, so fresh . . .'

Damn, thought Georgie. She whirled round to Mr Dickens who was, as she suspected, about to voice an objection. 'Eighty-four,' she said.

'Eighty-four,' repeated Dylan with another sob. 'The most sprightly pensioner I ever met.'

Jez was beginning to realize that all was not quite as it seemed. How could Dylan and Georgie possibly know someone he didn't know? This was decidedly fishy. 'Who's Lesley?' he reiterated, this time in a whisper.

Dylan put his arm round Jez's shoulders, gripping him

tightly, willing him to come to his senses. 'Governor,' he explained as he did so, 'Lesley was like an uncle –'

'Auntie –'

'– Lesley was like an auntie to this man. Look at him – he's so stunned he's become emotionally detached.'

Mr Dickens looked at Jez. He did seem to have retreated into himself; his face was a complete blank. Poor man, he thought. Denial is a terrible thing.

Dylan squeezed Jez's shoulder so hard that Jez winced with pain. Then he pressed his face against Jez's. 'LESLEY'S GONE!' he screamed. Then he slapped Jez, very hard, on the face.

'Owww!' Jez doubled over and buried his face in his hands.

'It's beginning to get through to him,' observed Dylan. He walloped Jez on the back. 'That's it, buddy – let it all out.'

Finally, the penny dropped. When Jez looked up he was crying, mainly, it has to be said, from extreme pain. But at least he understood what this was all about. His sobs intensified as he looked at Mr Dickens. 'Lesley,' he moaned. 'Not Lesley. Not poor, dear, darling Lesley. Not –'

'The cremation,' interrupted Georgie, 'is this morning.' She dabbed again with the handkerchief. 'I'm so sorry.'

Mr Dickens himself was nearly in tears. He cleared his throat and coughed uncomfortably. 'I, too, am sorry to hear of your loss.' He looked from Jez to Dylan. 'I have taken into account that you are to be paroled the day after tomorrow anyway – and have decided to allow you to attend the ceremony.'

Jez and Dylan rushed forward, leaned over the desk and kissed Mr Dickens's hand. This was far too much for the governor. He began to cry.

Georgie was nothing if not well-organized. At the gas-ometer, she had raided Jez and Dylan's respective ward-robes for two black suits. She had also borrowed other objects from their home (more of which in a minute) and, out of necessity, taken the Rover as well.

Ten minutes after the tearful interview with Mr Dickens, they were all standing outside the car, watching two guards give the vehicle a thorough search. All they found were several empty bags, carton upon carton of no-cow milk, two chewing gum wrappers and a sticker saying I LOVE BLENHEIM PALACE. They found no trace of two large metal suitcases. Dylan raised his eyebrows at Georgie. Enig-matic behind her dark glasses, she refused to be drawn.

Once the car had been given the all clear, the black-clad trio clambered inside. Georgie took the wheel. Jez sat beside her. Dylan languished in the back seat. Then one of the guards told him to move his feet to make room. 'We're not that daft, mate,' he said. 'If we let you go on your own, you'd scarper, wouldn't you?'

Behind her dark glasses, Georgie smiled enigmatically.

At the Crematorium

Lesley had evidently led a solitary life. There was no one else at the crematorium to mourn her passing into the other life, no tearful friends or distraught relations to weep and wail as she was burned to a cinder in the bowels of the building.

Georgie and her cohorts intended to make up for that. As the deferential vicar escorted them into the smallest chapel in the crematorium, she turned and addressed both him and the guard. 'Could you leave us for a short while?' she whispered.

The vicar nodded and turned away. The guard wasn't such easy meat. He looked on as the pathetic, slumped figures of Jez and Dylan made their way to the casket in the corner of the room. Then he looked at Georgie, at the tear-filled eyes and the pleading expression. 'All right,' he said. 'But I'll be right on the other side of the door.' He watched as Georgie joined the men at the coffin, held their hands in hers and sank to her knees. Then she started to cry. Jez and Dylan did likewise.

Embarrassed, the guard turned away and left the room.

As soon as she heard the door close behind him, Georgie snatched off her sunglasses and leaped to her feet.

'Right. We have absolutely no time to waste. Jez – open the coffin.'

'I can't do that to Lesley!' An adherent to the school of method acting, Jez was now firmly in character. Lesley was like an uncle – no, auntie – to him. How could he possibly desecrate her coffin?

'Oh, for heaven's sake!' Dylan sprang forward and lifted the coffin lid. He looked down in surprise at the peaceful face. 'Uncle,' he said.

'What?' Georgie was busy at the other end of the coffin.

'Auntie Lesley was a man after all.'

Georgie shrugged. 'Well, it's difficult to tell when they're eighty-four. They all get whiskery at that stage.' Then she rummaged about beside Auntie/Uncle Lesley's legs and extracted two large carrier bags. One of them contained three blow-up dolls. 'Hey,' said Dylan. 'Those are –'

'Yes, I know. I'm sorry, I stole them.' Georgie tipped the

deflated ladies onto the floor. Then she looked from Dylan to Jez. 'I didn't know you two were that lonely.'

Jez went pink. 'It's not what you think, Georgie. They were . . .'

But Georgie knew what they were. 'Yes, yes . . . a prize in a competition. Now get a move on . . . we have to get on with this.'

'With what?'

Georgie delved into the other bag and pulled out the soda stream and several gas canisters. 'Blow them up.'

'What?'

'We blow them up, put our clothes on them and then scarper.'

Jez beamed with delight. 'Georgie, you're a marvel!'

'And you've brought the money!' Dylan had just caught sight of the metal cases at the end of the coffin. Then he frowned. 'But where are Auntie Lesley's legs?'

'She doesn't have any.'

'Oh, poor thing. Eighty-four, no legs and sexually indeter-minate. No wonder she died.' Then Dylan lost interest in Auntie Lesley's lack of lower limbs and hauled the cases out of her coffin. 'You're a star, Georgie! We thought . . . well . . .'

'We thought you'd abandoned us.' Jez was almost in tears again.

Georgie looked affronted. 'Me? Abandon you?'

'After I told you about the . . . orphans.'

Georgie grinned. 'Well, you *are* orphans, aren't you? I admit I was a bit shocked at first but then I thought . . .' Georgie shrugged and picked up a doll. God forgive me, she prayed. I've turned into a criminal. I'm playing them at their own game. And I've sawn Auntie Lesley's legs off.

185

She hoped God would remember that Lesley had been dead at the time.

Working like fury, they changed into jeans and T-shirts from the carrier bags, dressed the now voluptuous dolls in their mourning clothes and closed the coffin. Then Georgie delved again into one of her bags, producing three of the plastic dancing plants that had so alarmed her on her first visit to the gasometer. She also extracted the headphone and speaker sets last used in the InfoTec scam.

'What on earth?' asked Jez.

Georgie handed him some insulation tape. 'Tape the plants to the dolls' faces.'

'What?'

'Just do it!'

Jez did it.

When he had finished, Georgie placed a small speaker and a microphone beside one of the kneeling dolls. Eyes shining, she looked up at her accomplices. 'Right, let's go!'

Following her lead, they grabbed the suitcases and ran out of the side entrance of the chapel and towards the parked Rover. 'I'm sorry I lied,' panted Jez as they sprinted, 'by not lying. I'm sorry.'

'Don't be.' Georgie didn't want to tread that particular conversational route again. She sprinted to the Rover and opened the boot. Then she threw in the carrier bags she had taken from the chapel and turned to Dylan. 'Open the cases.'

'What?'

'Open the cases. I mean, they're great – but hardly subtle. Put the money in the carrier bags instead.'

'Georgie,' sighed Jez. 'You've thought of everything!'

Indeed I have, thought Georgie. Absolutely everything.

But she hadn't paused to think what two million pounds, cash, might look like when she saw it. She gasped when Dylan opened the cases. Each was full to the brim with wads of fifty-pound notes. Wads and wads and wads. She could hardly believe her eyes.

Nor could Jez and Dylan. They had truly believed that they would never see the money again. Now here it was. Their eyes shone as they stared at row upon row of unflattering and defamatory likenesses of the Queen. They stared, mesmerized, at the money. Then they turned and grinned at each other.

'Stately . . .'

'. . . home!'

'What?' Georgie whirled round. 'What *are* you on about?'

'Oh . . . nothing.' Jez reached into one of the cases. 'C'mon. Into the bags and into the boot.'

It took them precisely thirty seconds to transfer the money. Thirty seconds after that, they were roaring out of the crematorium gates to freedom.

But why had they taped dancing plants to the blow-up dolls? And why had Georgie placed a speaker and mike in front of them? And why, in the car, were they now wearing headphones and mikes? The answer is that Georgie really had thought of everything.

The prison guard, suspicions aroused by how long they were taking to pray and wail and generally mourn the passing of Auntie Lesley, popped his head round the chapel door a few minutes after they had left the building.

He was reassured by the sight that greeted him. The three black-clad figures, racked by anguished sobs, were rocking to and fro – exactly as they had been a few minutes previously. 'Are you okay?' he asked.

His voice travelled via the mike to the headphones in the Rover. It was Dylan who responded. 'Just a few more minutes, please,' he wept. Then, as they sped through the countryside, they moaned even louder. Their sobs carried through the speaker in the chapel to the guard's ears. And as the wailing reverberated around the little room, the plants responded by dancing with renewed intensity. The surprised-looking blow-up dolls to whom they were taped had no choice but to respond to the rhythm. They rocked back and forth, ever faster, ever harder.

The sound of the guard closing the chapel door floated back to the speeding Rover. Jez removed his headphones. 'Good. We've got a few more minutes.'

'Where,' asked Dylan, 'are we going?' Now that he had recovered both his money and his spirits, he was more than a little concerned that Georgie was in complete control of the situation.

'There's a chess set,' lied Georgie, 'that's expected to go for about one million eight hundred thousand pounds.'

'Brilliant!' Dylan forgot his concerns. 'We buy it with the cash, then we resell . . . yes, yes!'

Jez leaned forward in the back seat. 'Georgie, this is wonderful! You're wonderful . . . you're great!'

But Georgie knew that she was a duplicitous cow and she was beginning to loathe herself for being such. Still, as Nanny had always said, *You have to finish what you started*.

And Nanny always knew best.

Yet there was no going anywhere for the moment. Much to the consternation of her passengers, Georgie was pulling to a halt.

'Why're you stopping?' asked Jez from the back seat.

'Look.'

They looked. In front of them was a combine harvester, slewed at a precarious angle across the road, blocking both carriageways.

'Shit!' said Jez.

'Christ,' said Dylan. 'This isn't happening.' So near, he thought, yet so far. It didn't look as if the peculiar farming machine thingy was going anywhere in a hurry. He turned round to Jez. 'What do we do now?'

But Jez had whipped on his headphones again. Back at the crematorium, the vicar had opened the chapel door and was explaining that he was terribly sorry but there was an unscheduled dog to deal with.

Jez frowned. 'An unscheduled dog?'

'What?' Georgie and Dylan looked at him in concern.

'Turn back. I've just heard the vicar say he had to fit in an unscheduled dog.'

'For cremation?'

'I suppose so.' Then, for good measure, Jez wailed a bit into his microphone.

Dylan looked put out. 'What about Auntie Lesley?' he asked. 'Doesn't she deserve a good cremation?' He had become rather fond of the idea of Auntie Lesley and didn't like the thought of her being usurped by some mongrel.

'We've got to get back,' urged Jez. 'Then we can make another plan.'

'But forwards is the way to freedom!'

'Think of the dog, Dylan.'

With an enigmatic smile, Georgie slammed the car into reverse.

They knew they were pushing their luck. (So, you'll be thinking, is the person who thought up this bit of plot.) Still, there was a chance they might just get away with it.

They did. Just. Tearing back into the chapel via the side door, they seized the nodding blow-up dolls and opened their valves. The dolls started to hiss, a sound that altered the tempo of the dancing plants. The spirited Dance of the Sugar Plum Fairies slowed into Dying Swan mode as they flailed and flapped and finally withered and ground to a halt.

Stripped, the blow-up dolls were stuffed ignominiously back into paper bags. But the dolls proved more resistant. Although they could do nothing about being deprived of their mourning garb, they stubbornly refused to deflate completely. In a panic, Jez and Dylan picked up two of them and hugged them to their breasts, literally squeezing the life out of them. Georgie went one better. She whipped a penknife out of her pocket and stabbed the third doll, repeatedly, all over its body. (This entire scenario was witnessed by Greta the crematorium cleaner as she poked her head through the little window. But Greta was Swedish and nothing could disrupt the stoic calm with which she approached both life and death. Humming her favourite ditty about fish and suicide, she went back to her mop.)

Then disaster struck. The door opened and the vicar and the guard stepped in. Jez and Dylan were still only half-dressed, Auntie Lesley's coffin was still open – and the bags of money were still lying on the floor.

It was Georgie, again, who saved the day. She hurled herself backwards against the guard and pressed the back of one hand against her forehead. For good measure, and just in case the guard thought she was attacking him, she offered an explanation. 'I'm swooning,' she said.

The guard nearly swooned as well. It wasn't every day a beautiful girl hurled herself backwards onto him. Normally this sort of activity was undertaken by ugly men. He stumbled under the sudden weight, bashed against the vicar and backed out of the door again.

Georgie waved a desperate foot at the bags of money. Dylan and Jez didn't need the hint. They bent down and threw the bags and the now wizened dummies into Auntie Lesley's coffin. Then they slammed the lid shut, finished dressing and, disguising their breathlessness with long sighs of despair, cast their last, lingering glances at the dear departed.

Georgie, the vicar and the guard were now back in the chapel. Still thrashing about (rather too energetically) in the confused aftermath of her swoon, Georgie stumbled against Dylan. This was deeply unwise. Caught off-balance, Dylan fell back against the control panel beside the coffin. A little red light began to flash.

The vicar was the only person in the room with an immediate understanding of what was happening. As sombre music began to echo throughout the chapel, he whipped out his Bible and began to extol the virtues of Auntie Lesley. The button was the automatic ceremony starter.

Dylan looked at Jez. Jez looked at Dylan. Then they both looked at Auntie Lesley's coffin and let out a piercing scream. Auntie Lesley was disappearing. A motor was humming beneath her coffin, whisking her off to the incinerator underneath the building.

'*No!*' Jez and Dylan rushed to the coffin. 'No, no, no!'

The guard had never seen anything like it. His heart went out to his charges as they grappled with the heavy lid. Then he stepped forward and put his hands on their shoulders. 'It's okay,' he soothed. 'It's okay. Sometimes you've just got to let your loved ones go.'

But Jez and Dylan were way beyond consolation. Distraught to the point of dementia, they shook, sobbed, wailed and wept as Auntie Lesley disappeared from view. Like an Egyptian Pharaoh, she was taking her riches with her. Admittedly, she couldn't take her legs, but she did have compensation for that inconvenience. She was going to her grave with three blow-up dolls, three dancing plants, a set of headphones – and two million pounds.

12

The journey back to prison was the most painful anyone in the car had ever undertaken. The prison guard was so affected by the final scene in the chapel that he let Jez and Dylan sit together in the back. He sat in the passenger seat beside Georgie, snivelling into the lace handkerchief she had kindly lent him. Georgie stayed silent and enigmatic behind her veil and dark glasses. Jez and Dylan, however, spent half the journey sobbing on each other's shoulders, the other half in stunned, disbelieving silence.

The guard felt that he had known Auntie Lesley well. How good she had been, he thought. How kind and generous. How spirited and sprightly. And how tragic it was that she had been snatched away from her loved ones at such a tender age. By the time they reached the prison Georgie's handkerchief was soaking wet. He offered it back to her as she drew to a halt outside the main gates. Georgie recoiled in horror. Then she leaned over and whispered, 'Keep it. Please. Auntie Lesley would have wanted you to have it.' She patted his knee. 'You've been so kind – have it as a memento.'

The guard sniffed his thanks and, not trusting himself to speak, opened his door. Behind him, Jez and Dylan did likewise. They couldn't care what happened to them now. Their lives were in ruins.

Georgie got out of the car as well. 'I'll pick you up the day after tomorrow,' she said to their retreating backs. 'Twelve noon?'

Neither man looked round. It was the guard who replied. 'Twelve noon,' he agreed. 'I'll make sure they're there. And . . . er, thank you.' He offered a brave smile and a small wave with his lace handkerchief.

Georgie inclined her head. 'Not at all.' Then she addressed the retreating backs once again. 'I'm sorry,' she called out. 'I'm really, really sorry.'

But the retreating backs retreated into the prison.

Georgie *was* sorry. They had looked so sad, so forlorn, so helpless. So *orphaned*. She really shouldn't have done it, she reflected. She shouldn't have been such a duplicitous cow. Then she consoled herself by opening the boot and looking at the large paper bags nestling inside. Two million pounds stared back at her.

Auntie Lesley wasn't such a Pharaoh after all. And her coffin, as it burned merrily to cinders, began to emit a rather unpleasant odour. The smell was partly attributable to Lesley's burning flesh, partly to the blow-up dolls and dancing plants – but mainly to the two hundred little portions of no-cow milk buried beneath the wads of shredded newspaper in her paper bags. Auntie Lesley was going to have an interesting afterlife.

So was Georgie. The following day (well, that counts as the afterlife) she made a few more phone calls. One was to the friendly vicar (who wasn't a vicar at all, but the gardener at the foundation) to thank him for helping with the fictitious funeral. The other was to the equally obliging farmer who had blocked the road with his combine harvester. Then, her thank yous completed (Nanny would have been delighted), she left the house for Mr Collyns's office, a bulging paper bag under each arm. Floss and Robin grinned madly as they waved good-bye. Now fully acquainted with her plans, they knew their troubles would soon be over.

When Georgie reached the office she marched, grimly determined, straight up to his secretary. 'I want to see Mr Collyns. Now.'

'Oh?' Clarinda invested the word with eight syllables, the first of which was *eau*. 'I think not,' she continued with a patronizing little smirk. 'Mr Collyns is busy at the moment.'

'Good,' snapped Georgie. 'Now he can be busy with me.' Leaving Clarinda open-mouthed with horror, Georgie stalked off down the corridor to Mr Collyns's inner sanctum. She threw the door open and stormed into the opulent office. And then, like Clarinda, she stared in open-mouthed horror. Mr Collyns was standing in the middle of the room, a smile on his face and a friendly arm round the shoulders of another man.

'Roger!'

But Roger was also trapped in the open-mouthed department. This was horrible. Awful. Horrified-silence-inducing.

'Hello,' said Mr Collyns. Like Clarinda, before she had become horrified, he was smirking.

Georgie looked from one man to the other. What on earth? Mr Collyns was *her* lawyer. Roger had never even met him. Something fishy was going on.

And then she remembered the paper bags and cared not a whit about fishiness. She was here on business. She would conduct her business and then she would never have to see Mr Collyns, or indeed Roger, ever again. 'I have the money,' she said to the former. 'For the foundation.'

Mr Collyns looked at Roger. Then he bowed his head – mainly to hide another smirk from Georgie. 'I'm sorry. I held him off as long as I could. I –'

'What have you done?' Georgie's heart missed several beats.

Mr Collyns looked up again. 'I had to sell him your house.'

At last Roger found his voice. And with it a smirk. 'And that means that the foundation will sadly be shut.'

Georgie gasped. Now she knew exactly how Jez and Dylan had felt about Auntie Lesley bolting off to the incinerator. 'You sold him my house?'

Mr Collyns looked away.

'You buggered a property deal that would have made us richer than you could have imagined,' snapped Roger.

'A property deal? A *property deal?*' squeaked Georgie. 'Christ, Roger, I've known you since I was a child. Has money ever meant anything to me?'

No, thought Roger. That was your major flaw.

Georgie's shoulders slumped. She felt suddenly sad

rather than angry. 'I honestly thought our marriage would work, I didn't love you – you knew that – but I thought I understood you. What little there was,' she added with a nasty glint in her eye, 'to understand. But, oh boy, you've really surpassed yourself, managing to keep a secret for . . . Christ!' Now the anger surfaced. 'You've been proposing to me for years! Is that what you had in the back of your mind?'

Roger shuffled from one beautifully shod foot to another. ''Course not. I only met the businessmen two months ago. It was a once in a lifetime deal.' As he spoke, he transferred his gaze from Georgie to Mr Collyns.

Georgie looked at the lawyer through narrowed eyes. The penny dropped. One didn't just *meet* such people by happy coincidence. 'You!' she sighed. 'Well . . . there had to be some brains behind the operation. We trusted you, you know. You've been our family lawyer since the dark ages.'

Mr Collyns looked suitably abashed. But only for a few seconds. Really, he thought, how naive she is. Family lawyer? *Trust?* The girl wasn't right in the head.

Georgie turned back to Roger. Her mouth was set in a thin, hard line and her eyes blazed. 'Just sell me the house back. What use is it to you?'

Roger squared his shoulders. 'You made me look a bloody fool in front of my Important Friends.'

'That's very kind of you to say so, Roger, but in all fairness, a lot of the groundwork had been done for me.'

Ouch, thought Mr Collyns.

Roger stormed out of the room.

Then Georgie rounded on the lawyer. 'Mr Collyns – you're sacked.'

Mr Collyns smirked again. 'From dealing with your property?'

The cruel jibe cut through Georgie like a knife. She turned on her heel and stalked out of the room.

'Hey ho,' said Mr Collyns to himself. 'Such is life.' Then, smirking, he sat down at his desk and buzzed on his intercom.

'Clarinda?'

'Yes, Mr Collyns?'

'Could you make out an invoice to Roger Grandison?'

'Certainly, Mr Collyns. For how much?'

'Oh . . . say, half a million?'

'Certainly, Mr Collyns.' Oh goody, thought Clarinda. He's rich as well as good-looking. I'll pout a little harder next time he visits.

Georgie Makes Another Mistake

Georgie was desperate. Standing in the street outside Mr Collyns's office, she looked at her watch and started to panic. It was eleven o'clock. In precisely two hours' time the wads of fifty-pound notes in her bags would cease to become legal tender. What to do? How to justify walking into a bank and asking to change them? It wasn't as if she had proof of just selling something. No handy receipt for two million, cash, was lurking in her handbag.

She dashed home to Chelsea.

Floss and Robin were devastated at her news. 'You mean that *shit* has swiped the house from under our feet? At the eleventh hour?'

'Well . . . I always said that punctuality was his thing.'

But Georgie's smile failed to reach her eyes. And she failed to conceal her desperation from Robin. He was the one most affected by Roger's behaviour – yet he was the one most sanguine about their current situation.

'We'll think of something,' he said. 'Let's just remain calm.'

'*Calm?*' shrieked Floss. 'We've got until one o'clock before the money turns to wallpaper.'

Georgie rolled her eyes. 'Thanks for clarifying that.'

In the corner of the sitting room, Robin had just thought of something. 'Why don't we spend the money on something Roger loves?'

'Roger only loves Roger. And even if he were for sale, I wouldn't buy him.'

'No, but Georgie, what about that horse of his? The one that's worth its weight in gold. Hoover Bag or something.'

'Vacuum Pack!' Georgie leaped to her feet. Then she rushed over to embrace her brother. 'Robin, you're a star! An absolute star! And I know the trainer. Stewart Pearson – remember him? He used to train some of Daddy's before . . . well . . . before . . .' Georgie left the rest of the sentence dangling in mid-air. There was no need to go into all that again. They all knew what she meant. Before Daddy died.

But there was another *before* that Georgie didn't know about. Stewart Pearson had indeed trained their father's horses – before he met Roger Grandison.

After he met Roger Grandison he realized that there was a lot more money to be made out of being duplicitous. So when Georgie phoned him to say that she was offering two million pounds for Roger's prized horse he didn't bat an eyelid. And by the time Georgie arrived at his yard he had Vacuum Pack all ready to go. He even lent Georgie a horsebox to transport him to another yard. Then he took her money, shook her hand and waved her good-bye.

Roger phoned Georgie an hour later. 'You bought the horse.' He seemed neither annoyed nor sad, just strangely distant.

But Georgie didn't notice. High on adrenaline, she punched the air with a fist, winked at her siblings and shouted down the phone. 'That's right! And I'm willing to exchange him for the house, the grounds and the foundation!'

A short silence at the other end – followed by words that were music to Georgie's ears. 'Okay. You win.'

Georgie whooped with delight. Then she frowned and pressed the phone closer to her ear. There was a strange sound reverberating down the line. It took her a few seconds to identify it: laughter. Roger's braying, hysterical laughter.

'I'm sorry,' he gasped after a moment. 'How rude of me. Georgie my love, I have something to tell you. I *authorized* the sale.'

'*What?*'

Another burst of uncontrollable laughter. Then, with evident difficulty, Roger managed to compose himself. 'Georgie – you've just paid two million quid for some dog food and wood glue.'

Dylan and Jez waited two hours for Georgie outside the prison. They wouldn't have waited so long had it not been for the guard from the previous day who kept trotting out to ply them with cups of tea and sympathetic insistence that Georgie would *definitely* arrive. 'You know what grief does to people,' he confided on one of his visits. 'They lose all track of time. Poor, poor Auntie Lesley,' he finished. Fearing that he might dissolve into tears at any moment, he trotted back into the prison, clutching Auntie Lesley's sodden legacy in his right fist.

'If that man mentions Auntie bloody Lesley once more I'm going to smack him in the face,' said Dylan.

'Then we'll end up back in prison.'

'Who cares?' Dylan had never felt so morose, so alone. In the time they had been waiting, every other prisoner being released that day had been picked up by one or two – and usually several – members of their families. Each joyful reunion served to remind Dylan and Jez that there was nobody out there for them. They were all alone in the world. They only had each other – and now the light had gone out of even that relationship. Five years, they both thought. Five years together and this is where we've ended up.

Eventually the prison guard took pity on them and, cursing Georgie, gave them money for a taxi home. 'Auntie Lesley would have wanted it this way,' he said.

Jez grabbed Dylan's right arm only just in time.

A surprise awaited them back at the gasometer. The empty metal cases – a hollow reminder of what they once had – were neatly arranged near the front door. A note was pinned to one of them. Jez picked it up. 'Jez,' he read aloud, '*I don't really care that you weren't giving the money away. I suppose I knew – but I hated being lied to. Maybe that's exactly what I've been doing. Maybe I can explain it all to you sometime. Love, Georgie.*'

'Ahh,' said Dylan. 'Isn't that nice. She still wants to explain. We can all meet up and talk about old times . . . like the time when she came up with this ingenious way of getting rid of two million pounds. What,' he added as he stomped around in fury, 'was this stroke of financial genius? Spend it? Invest it? Start up a chain of fast food outlets for dogs? No – she CREMATED IT! Christ, only in England, man, I'm telling you. Only in the good ol' U crap of K!'

'It wasn't her fault. It was a good plan.'

Beetroot with rage, Dylan rounded on his friend. 'I know! I know! I'm just being an asshole!'

True, thought Jez. Then he read the note again, and to himself. What did she mean by *maybe that's what I've been doing. Maybe I can explain*? Jez didn't quite like it – there was something fishy going on.

Or rather, something fishy had been going on. And it didn't really matter any more. Nothing mattered any more.

Dylan whirled round and glared at the suitcases. 'Exactly what does she think we're going to do with these anyway?'

'Well . . . I suppose she's just returning our property.'

A nasty look from Dylan. 'Well *isn't* that sweet.' He looked at the cases again; at the little red flashing lights on the locks. 'No, Jez, she's returned them because she thinks they might blow up.'

'Blow up?'

'Yes, that's what suitcases wired with explosives tend to do if you try and open them.'

'But why would she try to open them?' Jez frowned at the cases. 'They're –'

'THEY'RE EMPTY!' screamed Dylan. 'I know they're empty. Do you think I need reminding that they're empty?'

'So why . . . ?' But Jez never finished the sentence. He trailed off into silence, looking, as did Dylan, towards the front door. Someone was trying to break in. Judging by the force of the blows against the door, that someone wasn't alone. And that someone was screaming 'LITTLE BAS- TARDS!' over and over again. Jez and Dylan looked at each other. No Camilla Cash, this. Someone was taking the law into his own hands.

'Quick!' Dylan was already lifting the Persian carpet. 'It's the only place.'

Jez nodded and grappled with the rusty rivet. A moment later they were in the – now empty, but Dylan doesn't want to be reminded of that – floorsafe. As the lid banged down over their heads the intruders struck a final blow at the weakening front door. It crashed to the ground and the intruders stampeded into the gasometer.

James Stratton-Luce was at the head of the posse. Behind him was Dave Ray. And forming the body of the army were various residents of Cranworth Crescent – and Babs Ray. Babs's face was set in a thin, angry little line. She gave not a whit about the false arrest and subsequent pardon of her husband; she didn't care about the loft insu- lation scam. She was dismissive about her fellow intruders' complaints. Babs had her own agenda.

Missing *Blind Date* had been like having all her teeth pulled without an anaesthetic – yet she had, in time, recov- ered. Rearranging the crooked pictures had been just about bearable. But the São Paulo business had been the last straw. When Babs had discovered the off-hook receiver, she had shrieked in an outraged poodle sort of fashion and picked it up. She had been about to shriek again when she placed it next to her ear and heard the unmistakably foreign voice. Then, with a little frown, she listened a little harder. She recognized those gravelly tones, the knee-tremblingly seductive voice. The man caressing her with silken vowels was familiar to her, and so was the language he spoke. She would have bet her boudoir that he was Ricardo from her favourite Brazilian soap. She listened more carefully. Yes. Ricardo. A slow smile had spread across her painted features. When she discovered that the soap had been cancelled she had been suicidal. How could she survive Friday nights without Ricardo? Now, with this discovery, she wouldn't even have to wait until Friday night. Every night could be hers and Ricardo's. Every day. Every hour of every day if she so chose.

Babs had been ecstatic. She had even sent up a silent prayer of thanks to the intruder who had cruelly deprived her of *Blind Date*. And then, two months later, the phone bill arrived. Babs's ecstasy turned to agony and her knees trembled for quite a different reason. Three thousand pounds. How to justify that? How to explain the repeatedly dialled twenty-digit number to Dave? Even though she had put Ricardo on her Friends and Family list, he had still cost her a small fortune.

And then Babs had made an even more appalling discovery: she found that she was addicted to calling Ricardo. Try as she might, she found herself irresistibly drawn to the phone the minute Dave left the house. She had developed a secret and highly expensive little vice – and it was all the fault of the intruder. He had ruined her life.

So when Babs stomped into the gasometer in her poodle booties (minus the band of fur), she was bent on revenge. She was going to ruin the lives of the two men who lived here. Yet as soon as she was through the front door she stopped in her tracks, appalled by the vision in front of her. Mrs Gosling, hot on her heels, crashed into her. 'Common little piece,' she muttered to herself. Then she circumnavigated Babs and pounded into the body of the gasometer, wielding the shooting stick she had received on special offer (*such a snip!*) from *Country Living*.

But Babs remained frozen on the spot. She had never seen such a shrine to bad taste, such a monument to vulgarity. Surely no one with even a fleeting acquaintance with sanity could live in such a place? It took a huge amount of money to make a place look this cheap (Babs knew about things like that) and where had it got them? Precisely nowhere. As she surveyed the interior of the gasometer, she realized she was looking at a crime infinitely worse than the one she intended to commit. These men would have to be taught a lesson. A lesson in interior design.

On the journey to the gasometer Babs had initially harboured reservations about the purpose of their visit. Babs was nothing if not refined and she knew it simply wasn't done to break into someone's house and trash the place. That sort of activity was undertaken by people less principled than herself (Babs remained endearingly naive about the true source of her husband's income). Yet now, with her senses being assaulted from all sides, Babs realized that she would be doing a favour to whoever lived here if she helped redesign the interior. Her mouth happily reset in a thin, angry little line, she made her way over to the greenhouse in the corner, wielding the policeman's truncheon that Dave had so cleverly managed to acquire for that cops-and-robbers fancy dress party last year. (Babs had dressed as Calamity Jane, but that's another story. A very long and painful one.)

Underneath the pandemonium being meted out by the braying Sloanes and the common little pieces (Tracey Slattery had joined in the fray. Hell, after all, hath no fury like a strumpet scorned), Jez and Dylan cringed in the darkness of their hiding place. Every time they heard a crash they winced in pain. Every time they heard an object being hurled across the room they groaned with despair. And every time they heard a bray or a yelp they shuddered in silent grief for the lives being destroyed above them. Their lives.

The commotion lasted a good half hour. There was much to destroy. And the vengeance with which it was destroyed was intensified by the absence of the inhabitants. James Stratton-Luce had been confident of finding them at home. After all, they had just been released from prison. Where else would they go? Didn't normal people, under such circumstances, return home for a nice cup of tea? (Nice cups of tea, for James, belonged to the past. He was beginning to miss Eleanor, beginning to realize that she had had her uses. James had only just discovered the whereabouts of the kitchen at number one, Cranworth Crescent. He hadn't yet found out how it worked.)

When all was in smithereens, the breathless band of vigilantes stood and surveyed their work. Then they turned and smiled at each other. Mrs Furnival-Jones found herself smiling at Tracey Slattery. Mrs Gosling was to be seen grinning at Babs. There was nothing, the smiles seemed to say, like a shared interest to break the social ice. Babs leaned on her truncheon and felt a refined candlelit supper coming on, populated by these lovely people with double-barrelled names. She would invite Trixie and Mervyn. Then again, perhaps they would be intimidated by such class. Better to pass them off as servants.

Mrs Furnival-Jones found herself actually warming to Tracey Slattery. She had wielded that tennis racket with real panache. Fancy little people like Tracey playing a game like that! But then one should never judge by appearances, nor even accents. One should be broadminded about things like that. After all, one's tennis partner had just died (*so inconsiderate*) and one did want to win the cup. Perhaps Tracey and her husband should be invited round for dinner. Not, of course, the Royal Doulton (one didn't want to intimidate them). Yes, it was coming together. It was panning out most satisfactorily.

James Stratton-Luce and Dave Ray had their minds on higher things than supper or dinner. They were staring at the metal cases. 'Money?' suggested James.

'Money,' agreed Dave. Then he leaned forward and picked them up.

'Hey!' James was having none of that. 'One each, I'd say.'

Dave shrugged. He could always send Geoff round later to burgle the pompous git. 'Sure,' he said. 'One each.'

James grinned and bent down. Now that he had joined the criminal classes (*white collar* crime, of course) he was confident of finding an accomplice to send round for the other case. 'So,' he said to the room at large. 'All set?'

Everyone nodded and fell into formation behind James and Dave as they marched from the battlefield.

Dylan and Jez waited a good ten minutes before emerging from their hiding place. The sounds from the battlefield had filtered loud and clear into the safe. They were in no doubt that if they, the enemy, had shown themselves, they would have been beaten to a pulp.

But when they climbed out to survey the damage, they almost wished they had been destroyed along with all their worldly goods. Nothing, absolutely *nothing* was left intact. Every pane of the greenhouses had been broken. Every bean bag had been punctured. The leopard-skin chesterfield was in tatters. The whale had been drowned, the sculptures destroyed. Even worse, the furniture earmarked for the stately home was smashed to pieces. And so was Jez's beautiful cardboard model – the masterpiece that he had kept with him for eighteen years.

It was the last battered object that prompted a hollow laugh from both men. What had they been playing at? Why had they been nursing their silly Impossible Dreams for so long? Who did they think they were? And why had they thought life couldn't get any worse?

They sat down on the shredded sofa and burst into tears.

13

Well, this is all a little grim, isn't it? Nearly at the end of the story and not even a tad of hope in sight. Misery all round. And lest one think the vigilantes are happy – think again. Both James and Dave opened their cases the minute they reached their respective cars. The resultant explosions were spectacular and, for the men involved, fatal. Babs, investigating Mrs Furnival-Jones's availability for a refined candlelit supper, had been some way off and survived the blast. But she never recovered from her encounter with posh people and developed a fierce, lifelong antipathy towards them. The candlelit supper never materialized.

The inhabitants of Cranworth Crescent decided that

white collar crime hadn't been quite their thing after all. Smashing up gasometers was one thing – being frightened to death by the blast that had killed James was something else entirely. Anyway, they now had something else to occupy their minds. With James dead and Eleanor terminally bewildered, who would move into number one? They rushed back to Holland Park to form a management committee from which Tracey Slattery and her husband were excluded. One had learned one's lesson. Give that sort of person an inch and next minute they would be inviting you round to a refined candlelit supper.

Georgie Comes Clean

Dylan and Jez were crying in each other's arms when Georgie walked in. Oh, she thought, how *sweet*. Then she saw the carnage. 'Oh my God! Oh my God! So *that's* what they were doing? Oh how horrible.'

'Georgie!' Jez looked up in astonishment.

Dylan looked up through narrowed eyes. 'You mean you *saw* them – and you didn't try to stop them?'

'Well . . . there were about twenty of them.' Then Georgie smiled. 'Anyway, I don't think they'll be bothering you again.'

'Oh? Why?'

'Bang, bang,' said Georgie.

Dylan and Jez nodded. 'Ah. So they opened them. If people,' continued Dylan, 'weren't so greedy they wouldn't end up in such a mess.'

Georgie looked at the ground and shuffled uncomfortably. 'Um . . . you know how you were honest with me, Jez?'

'Mmm.'

'Well . . . I'd like . . . that is to say . . . um . . .' Georgie looked up again. 'The money didn't burn in the coffin.'

'*What?*' Dylan and Jez looked at her in utter amazement. Dylan was so amazed that he began to hyperventilate.

Georgie handed him a paper bag.

'Thanks.'

'My pleasure.'

'What on earth – ?' began Jez.

Georgie stalled him with an authoritative hand. 'My father,' she explained, 'converted one wing of our family's house into a foundation for people with Down's syndrome. My brother was born with Down's and – '

'Where's the money?' screamed Dylan through his bag. 'This is unbelievable!'

But Georgie was determined to tell them the whole story. 'Father died recently and the house and the grounds and the foundation had to go into receivership . . . we couldn't pay the death duties.'

Dylan's paper bag had done the trick. He threw it on the floor and glared at Georgie. 'You spent all our money on people with Down's syndrome?'

Jez, too, was aghast. 'We thought we'd lost all the money.'

'Yeah.' Dylan pointed an accusatory finger at Georgie. 'But she swindled us for a Good Cause.' Then he stood up and jabbed the finger into her face. 'WHAT WERE YOU THINKING OF?'

Georgie looked away. 'I wanted to buy the house – but I was too late.'

'SO WHAT DID YOU BUY?'

'Um ... you'd better ... er ... why don't you come outside?'

At the back of the gasometer was a patch of wasteland. Nobody could find any use for the patch which was, presumably, why it was referred to as a wasteland. Jez and Dylan had little interest in gardening and had never bothered to mow the grass that grew in sporadic but lush clumps all over the patch. The local children occasionally played football there and, once in a while, a tramp bedded down for the night on one of the lusher clumps. And that was the only activity ever witnessed by the wasteland.

Until today. Today the wasteland was playing host to Vacuum Pack. The horse was in seventh heaven. True, the surroundings were somewhat less than salubrious – but the food was both excellent and abundant. He chomped and mowed, happily unaware of the effect he was having on the two men emerging from the gasometer.

'I feel sick,' said Dylan in a dangerously quiet voice. 'We could have had some beautiful mansion where we all could live in luxury – albeit with a bunch of loonies.'

Georgie gasped.

'Sorry.' Dylan had the grace to look abashed. 'With disadvantaged children. Instead we've got a horse whose only value is as an Italian sausage.'

Vacuum Pack heard that. He looked up and cast a really filthy look in Dylan's direction.

'Er ... sorry ...' Dylan turned to Georgie. 'What's his name?'

'Vacuum Pack.'

'Well I'm sorry, Vacuum Pack, but that's the truth.'

No, it isn't, thought Vacuum Pack. Italian sausages tend to be made of pork. Imagine confusing me with a pig. Ignorant Yank. He snorted and resumed his chomping.

'Two million pounds,' whispered Dylan. 'Two million pounds for *that*.'

'He's not *that* bad,' said a defensive Georgie. 'He's entered for the Challenge Cup. It's the biggest race of the season.'

'Georgie! He's got about as much chance of winning as a blow-up doll. And talking of which, what happened to them? Did they burn or was that another of your little tricks?'

'They burned. With Auntie Lesley.'

'Who's Auntie Lesley?' The clear voice rang out from beside the bickering trio, surprising two of them.

But it didn't surprise Georgie. She turned round and, grinning, introduced Floss. 'You've met Jez, haven't you?'

'The toaster man? Yes. Hello again.'

'And this is Dylan.'

But this was Dylan as no one had ever seen him before. He couldn't move a muscle; couldn't utter a word. All he could do was stare at the vision of loveliness in front of him.

Georgie smiled and turned to Floss. To her intense surprise, her sister was aping Dylan. She couldn't move a muscle, couldn't utter a word. All she could do was stare at the vision of handsomeness in front of her.

'Well,' said Georgie. 'Both lost for words. Now *that's* pretty unusual.' Then she turned to the young man following in Floss's wake. 'This is Robin.' She turned to Jez. 'Our brother.'

Jez stepped forward and shook hands.

Dylan neither noticed Robin nor heard Georgie introduce

him. He had eyes only for Floss; his ears were assailed by a choir of angels belting out happy hymns, his head was full of kaleidoscopic visions of multiple happiness; all his other senses were similarly assaulted by . . . (Oh get on with it.)

'Dylan? Er . . . Dylan?'

'What?' Jez's voice hauled him back down to earth.

'Georgie's brother, Robin.'

'Ah.' Dylan smiled and shook hands. 'You're very lucky to have Floss for a sister.'

Robin burst out laughing. He knew Americans were prone to looking goofy – but this one took the biscuit. Still, he seemed pleasant enough. Robin gestured towards the gasometer. 'Nice place.'

'D'ya think so?' Dylan beamed. 'We like it.'

Floss, too, had snapped out of her daze. Robin's mention of Jez and Dylan's home reminded her of matters more urgent – although far less pleasant – than staring into Dylan's eyes. Roger had issued a decree that the foundation, and therefore Robin, had to be out of the house by noon the following day. She imparted the unhappy news to Jez and Dylan.

'I just can't believe,' said Georgie, 'that Roger is doing this.'

Robin shrugged. 'He's angry and he's scared of me and my friends.'

What a brave face he's putting on all this, thought Jez.

Dylan went one better. He turned back to Floss. 'We're going to save your brother,' he announced. 'And we're going to save your house.'

Jez looked appalled. Georgie looked doubtful. Robin looked politely hopeful. Floss grinned from ear to ear.

'How?' whispered Jez to his friend.

'Ma'am,' said the friend (we know to whom), 'don't you worry.'

Jez took Dylan by the arm and pulled him away from the others. ''Scuse me,' he muttered with an apologetic smile. 'Tactics.'

'Exactly how,' he snapped when they were out of earshot, 'are we going to save "Ma'am's" house? You've fallen. That's what's happened. You don't know what you're saying.'

'Well, you've fallen for Georgie.' Dylan was oddly defensive.

'That's different.'

'Why?'

'Because we know each other.'

'Well . . . Floss and I will get to know each other.'

Jez was deeply scathing. 'Would that be before or after you've saved her brother, her house, her grounds and her foundation?'

Dylan looked into the distance. 'There *has* to be a way. There's *got* to be something we can do.' Then he looked away from the distance to something altogether nearer. That something tried, too late, to pretend it wasn't there. It bent its head and began to mow the grass.

If I keep my head down, thought Vacuum Pack, I won't be able to see anyone. And so no one'll be able to see me.

Now we know why poor old Vacuum wasn't such a whiz on the racetrack.

'It's got to win the Challenge Cup,' said Dylan, walking back to the others to explain his plan. Vacuum joined them. After all, he reasoned, if they're going to discuss my fate, I might as well be there.

'Oh *please*,' said Jez.

Hey, thought Vacuum. I've got feelings too, you know.

'I have it!' Dylan patted Vacuum's flank. He turned to Floss. 'What makes a good horse win?'

'Good jockey?'

'Yeah – but what else?'

'Er . . . ground . . . fitness . . .'

'What else?'

'Fancying the horse in front?' hazarded Robin.

They all laughed. But Jez was the one who knew exactly how Dylan's mind worked. Lateral thinking. Egyptians and catapults. He turned to Dylan and grinned. 'A light jockey?'

'Exactly!'

Oh how thrillingly unoriginal, thought Vacuum. You'll have to come up with something better than that.

But Vacuum was unaware of the existence of the blow-up dolls.

So was Floss. As they repaired to the gasometer she was horrified, firstly by the mess and secondly by the fact that Jez and Dylan kept a stash of the pouting plastic creatures.

'How very quaint,' she said in glacial tones.

Dylan looked highly embarrassed. 'It's not what you think.'

'What is it, then?'

It was Georgie who explained. She drew Floss to one side and explained several of the aspects of Dylan and Jez's life she had yet to explain to Floss. She already knew about the money (or lack of). She was intrigued to find out about the competition mania. And she was horrified to learn of the reasons for the catastrophic mess in the gasometer.

'But supposing those people come back?' she wailed.

'Oh they won't. They're dead, you see.'

Floss breathed a sigh of relief. 'Well, thank God for small

mercies. At least that's one less problem to worry about.'
Then, seeking further reassurance, she bent closer to her
sister. 'Are you absolutely sure about the dolls?'

'Absolutely. Brownies' honour.'

'You were expelled from the Brownies.'

'For honourable reasons.'

'Mmm.' Floss looked over to Dylan. He was in the process of unwrapping a blow-up doll.

Georgie followed her gaze. 'Whatever he's up to, you can
be sure it's original.'

Dylan's Plan

The Jockey Club – the regulatory body of the racing frater-
nity – reckoned it had seen it all. The members of its
Security Committee were alert to all the race-rigging scams
known to man. And every year, a week after the publication
of the latest Dick Francis, they met to discuss the fruits
of their year's research into the latest methods by which
criminals might seek to thwart them and break their rules.
They sat around an antique table and compared their
(remarkably similar) notes. The year's scam, they con-
cluded, would be perpetrated by a wealthy businessman
with psychotic tendencies and thwarted by an ex-jockey-
turned-private-investigator. It would involve a subplot that
had something to do with diamonds or smuggling. A pretty
girl would appear and, after being exposed to danger for a
bit, would fall for the man doing the thwarting. There might
also be a princess of indeterminate nationality swanning
about being imperious. There might even be a stately home,
lurking and decaying in the background. One thing was for

sure: this year's scam was pretty damn rip-roaring and they simply couldn't wait for next year's. A dashed shame, all in all, that there was only one a year.

Had any members of this august committee admitted to an acquaintance with blow-up dolls, they might have been able to envisage a plot along the lines of which Dylan was working. 'Floss,' he said over his shoulder as he grappled with his doll. 'Do you know any tame jockeys?'

'As opposed to wild ones, you mean?'

Dylan grinned. Dylan was already so smitten he would have grinned at Floss painting a fence.

'I know one,' said Georgie with a glint in her eye. 'Charlie Panfield. He's the sweetest man in the world. And,' she finished, missing Jez's piqued look, 'he hates Roger.'

'Great!'

'Uh . . . Dylan?'

'Yes.'

'Are you going to share this with us?'

'Share what?'

Georgie sighed. 'Whatever it is you're plotting.'

'Sure, babe. When's this Challenge Cup?'

'Tomorrow.'

'Then can you come back first thing in the morning with your tame jockey. Er . . . all of you?' As he turned, his look embraced Georgie and her siblings – but it lingered on Floss.

'Sure,' said Georgie. 'Er . . . what about you, Jez?' She looked round the ruined gasometer. 'Staying here?'

'Yes,' grinned Jez. 'It's my plan as well.'

Ah, so that's why the plan was reluctant to divulge itself.

Jez and Dylan's Plan

The plan was audacious. The members of the Security Committee of the Jockey Club would probably have abandoned Dick Francis and commissioned a novel from Jez and Dylan had they known about it. But they would never know, for the plan was going to succeed.

The blow-up doll was only part of it. It was going to act as a sort of parachute that, once inflated, would lift Charlie Panfield off the saddle and enable Vacuum Pack to race ahead. But poor old Vacuum needed more help than that – he needed Jez's part of the plan as well.

Again, this involved weight, and would come into play even before the race began. If they made Charlie Panfield appear heavier than he really was, then he would be able to dispense with some of the weights in his saddle. Here's the plan in action.

At the Races

A grinning Charlie Panfield walked into the weighing-in room. He was delighted with the plan and had agreed to it with alacrity. In his book, any chance to make a fool out of Roger Grandison was to be snapped up (although, like Georgie, he agreed that much of the groundwork had been done already). And then there was Vacuum Pack to think of: Charlie had been fond of the animal and livid at the cavalier way he had been abandoned. There was a third, less altruistic reason why Charlie had jumped at the idea put forward by Georgie that morning: if he won the

Challenge Cup, his career would soar upwards faster than an inflatable doll.

Charlie stood and waited for his turn to be weighed. In front of him, another jockey was sitting on the chair bolted to the giant set of scales. The steward waited for the dial on the scales to settle. It did so at eight stone, seven pounds. 'Seven pound handicap,' he said to the jockey. Then he handed him several flat lead weights to insert into his saddle.

Charlie's heart began to race as he stepped forward to take his place on the chair. The grinning steward noticed neither the little dial hidden in his clenched fist nor the hefty *thud* as his left boot made contact with the plate of the scales. 'Now, Panties,' he said, looking at the scrawny little chap. 'Big handicap for you by the looks of things. You ought to eat a bit more, y'know.'

Oh dear, thought Charlie. Then he turned the dial in his hand, altering the magnetic field on the plate soldered to his left boot. The pointer on the larger dial above him shot off the scales.

The steward's eyes nearly popped out of his head. 'Eighty-five stone? Nah,' he said, tapping the scales. 'Something wrong here.'

There was. The magnetic field was so strong it was pulling Charlie downwards; his left boot was trying to bolt to the bowels of the earth. Charlie winced in pain and turned the dial again. The pressure decreased – and with it, his weight. He lost seventy-six stone in three seconds.

'That's better,' said the relieved steward. 'But you're still heavier than you look.'

'It's my heart,' said Charlie in a feeble attempt at humour.

'Your heart?'

'Yeah. I'm on Vacuum Pack.'

'Ah.' The steward nodded in sympathy. His own heart would have sunk to his boots (geddit?) had he been in Charlie's position. 'Well,' he said with a smile, 'if it's any consolation, you can take off four pounds.'

It was a huge consolation. Charlie should have been putting on the weights, not dispensing with them.

He walked out of the weighing-in room and surveyed the packed stand above him. He'd never seen the place so crowded, never felt such palpable tension in the air. And then he shielded his eyes from the sun and peered up at the owners' and trainers' enclosure. There was an air of palpable smugness emanating from a man in a beautifully cut yellow jacket. Roger Grandison.

Roger felt he had a right to feel exceedingly smug. The windfall two million from Georgie's ludicrous purchase had been put to good use: he had bought Remote Control, today's favourite for the big race. Not only had he done that, he had been left with change – enough to cover the money he had shelled out for the wedding. Roger was feeling awfully pleased with himself.

So, standing beside him, was Mr Collyns. He had just phoned Clarinda at the office and instructed her to tear up the invoice she had written to Mr Grandison. Clarinda had responded with a suspicious 'Eau?', followed by a 'Why?' Then she went over the moon when her boss replied that he wanted to replace it with another, larger invoice. Mr Grandison was obviously even richer than they had initially thought. Clarinda replaced the receiver and practised her pout. Mr Collyns toyed with the cash register in his head.

Then Roger roused him from his reverie with a burst of laughter.

'What is it?'

Roger laughed again. 'Georgie. She's come to watch her dog food run. Poor little thing. It almost makes one feel sorry for her.' Almost, but not quite. Georgie had, after all, made him look foolish in front of his Very Important Friends.

He called out to her as she made her way into the enclosure. 'Good luck, you old filly!' Then he roared with laughter again. Really, he was on such tremendous form. A horse guaranteed to win; a tame lawyer whom he had no intention of paying; oodles of champagne to look forward to drinking and, of course, cohorts of New and Important Friends to make when he'd won the race. Roger sighed with pleasure and sank into self-adulating silence.

Georgie ignored his taunt. Flanked by Dylan and Jez, she sat down several rows in front of him. She was practically shaking with nerves. This was it. They had done all they could. The rest was in the lap of the gods – whichever gods were responsible for luck, dishonesty and blow-up dolls. She turned to Jez. 'Are you sure this'll work?'

'It'll work.' Jez spoke with more confidence than he felt. It *should* work, he told himself as he fingered the remote control in his pocket. With a little luck, a lot of dishonesty and perfect timing.

The torso of the blow-up doll was secreted in the lining of Charlie Panfield's silk jacket. Her head, they had decided, would have to go. With no dancing plants in the equation it was redundant and, like her limbs, too bulky. She had been reduced to nothing more than a bag with a cylinder attached. And that cylinder contained helium gas. She wasn't going to know what had hit her when Jez activated the remote control.

A minute later a profound silence embraced the entire racecourse as the commentator announced the start of the Challenge Cup. This was the most important event in the racing calendar, the most prestigious, the one on which reputations and fortunes rested. More money would change hands here today than at any other race in the country. This was the race that had the Security Committee of the Jockey Club on the edge of their seats, scouring the stadium for a villain, a hero, a princess of indeterminate nationality, a pretty girl in danger and a well-researched subplot.

'And they're off!' yelled the commentator at the sound of the starting pistol. 'The thirty-fourth Challenge Cup is off and running! Wyndoms Grace takes the lead from the favourite Remote Control . . . two lengths behind them comes Tender Moments . . . and as they pass the first furlong it's Wyndoms Grace from Monterey Fire, Remote Control, Tender Moments and . . . and Vacuum Pack!'

Below him, Roger frowned. Vacuum Pack had no business being up there with the leaders. Still, no need to worry. Georgie had probably told him to imagine he was being chased by dog food manufacturers. They'd catch him in the end.

In the front row, Vacuum's new owners sat on the edge of their seats. This was going better than expected – and they hadn't used the helium yet.

'And at the fourth furlong it's Wyndoms Grace still in the lead from Vacuum Pack and Remote Control! And as they come to the fifth furlong Wyndoms Grace is tiring . . . Old Whisky just a head in front of Vacuum Pack and necking with Wyndoms Grace . . .'

Roger began to sweat. He lowered his binoculars. 'Vacuum's an old puffer – I can't bloody believe this!' Then, murder in his eyes, he turned to Mr Collyns. 'You told me to sell him!'

Oh dear, thought Mr Collyns. Better phone Clarinda again.

'Vacuum Pack,' screamed the commentator, 'has a lot of life in him still. So too has Old Whisky . . . Old Whisky takes the lead from Vacuum Pack and, a long way back now, Wyndoms Grace.'

Dylan nearly fell off his seat as he trained his binoculars on the thundering horses. Beside him, Jez extracted the remote control. 'Wait,' hissed Dylan. 'Not yet . . .'

'And as they come round the final bend it's Old Whisky from Vacuum Pack . . . and into the home stretch . . .'

'. . . And helium!' yelled Dylan.

Jez hit the button.

Vacuum Pack had been told what they were going to do. His initial reservations about Dylan evaporated as the plan was outlined. This, reckoned Vacuum, was better than any-thing he'd heard of before. And it had most of the right ingredients. With Georgie as the pretty girl, Roger as the wealthy villain and, of course, himself as the hero, Vacuum reckoned it made for a damn fine plot. A film, even? Vacuum thought he would come over rather well on celluloid.

Just as he was mulling over what to do about the lack of a princess of indeterminate nationality, Vacuum remembered where he was. Best keep running, he told himself.

And then he realized that Jez had hit the button and that Charlie Panfield was rising above the saddle. To everyone watching the race, it looked as if a gust of wind had inflated Charlie's jacket. No one suspected foul play in the shape of a dismembered blow-up doll.

Vacuum was delighted. With a weight off his shoulders and his mind (he'd decided that Floss could be the princess) he shot ahead.

'And Vacuum Pack,' yelled the over-excited commentator, 'is now giving head to Old Whisky and as they race for the line it's Vacuum Pack from Old Whisky . . . Vacuum Pack takes Old Whisky from behind . . . Vacuum Pack . . . it's Vacuum Pack!'

Grinning like mad, Vacuum sprinted over the line a head in front of Old Whisky.

The racecourse erupted. Pandemonium ruled. The stand and enclosures reverberated with shock, disbelief, amazement and thunderous applause. Never before in the annals of British racing had something like this happened. Never had a complete outsider romped past the favourite to the post to win the Challenge Cup.

Georgie, Jez and Dylan went berserk. They leaped up and down, they hugged each other, they screamed with delight and they punched the air with glee. They'd done it: the gods had reached into their laps and hurled luck, dishonesty and a blow-up doll past the post.

Jez himself nearly forgot about the blow-up doll. Vacuum and Charlie, he suddenly noticed with horror, were still charging down the racetrack; Charlie's jacket was still billowing out behind him. With a guilty start, Jez pressed the remote control again. Below him, Vacuum slowed down and Charlie sank gratefully back into the saddle.

Above him, Roger punched Mr Collyns smack in the face, sending him reeling to the ground.

Then Dylan put his arms round his companions. 'To the winner's enclosure!'

Vacuum Pack and Charlie Panfield were in their respective elements. The latter was grinning broadly and contemplating the successful career ahead of him. The former, adopting the vaguely disdainful sneer common to celebrities, was envisaging the life of luxury ahead of him. No more racing – he was far too valuable for that. No, no, Vacuum was going to be a stud. He would swan around the country, 'covering' (now there was a euphemism if ever he'd heard one) all the prettiest mares. In between times, he would rest in the most luxurious stables, partake of the choicest of foods and do just enough exercise to keep himself in shape. And no more of that nasty running business, thank you very much.

As Charlie and Vacuum continued their triumphant circuit round the ring, a throng of excited racegoers appeared. Amongst them were Dylan, Jez and Georgie, being pestered on all sides by clamouring owners. 'We'll pay a stud fee of a hundred and fifty thousand guineas!' yelled one to Dylan.

'I know Vacuum is a recent purchase,' pleaded another, tugging at Jez's arm. 'But I'm sure we could pay you more than you laid out.'

'I want that horse,' said a Saudi prince to Georgie. 'Name your price.'

Georgie turned and grinned at them all. 'Thank you. Thank you all.' Then she addressed the sheepish-looking individual at the rear of the throng. 'Roger? Any offers?'

Roger swallowed the lump in his throat – and with it his pride. 'The house,' he mumbled. 'And a hundred thousand.'

Georgie's hand tightened on Jez's arm. 'Three –'

'Five hundred thousand,' interrupted Dylan.

A small blood vessel ruptured on Roger's perfect nose. Then he looked at the Important People all around him. He couldn't possibly climb down in front of them. He took a deep breath. 'Okay. Done.'

'Oh.' Georgie had suddenly remembered something. 'And the Rolls, please.'

Roger winced. The Rolls. He loved his Rolls. It made him look so important. Then he looked over at Vacuum. Well, he would just have to sell the brute on again and buy another Rolls with the proceeds. He turned back to Georgie. 'All right. The Rolls as well.'

Dylan sprang forward, striking while the iron was piping hot. He waved a bunch of papers in front of the scowling Roger. 'Now, I'm going to need you to sign here . . . and here . . . and here.'

Roger bit his lip and signed there and there and there.

Vacuum Pack watched him with a baleful expression. Oh God, he thought. So much for the life of Riley. Then he remembered who he was, remembered that he was the winner of the Challenge Cup. Roger couldn't possibly afford to mistreat him. Roger would have to be extra nice to him.

When Roger had signed the papers he beetled off in pursuit of the Saudi prince. Vacuum's spirits lifted even further. He rather liked the idea of the prince; the man was famous for keeping his horses in the lap of luxury. Vacuum had heard rumours of swimming pools and the finest medical facilities in the equine world. Vacuum was, he suspected, going to live Happily Ever After.

As the crowd melted away, a man came up to Georgie and shook her hand. 'Well done,' he said. 'Absolutely marvellous race, Lady Georgina.'

Jez and Dylan spun round as the man walked off. '*Lady Georgina?*'

Georgie looked embarrassed. 'Oh . . . yes. Er, I forgot to mention that. Are you cross?' Her last words were addressed solely to Jez.

Jez looked at her for a moment. A slow smile spread across his face. Then he shook his head and drew Georgie into his arms.

Dylan grinned as he watched. Then he shook his head and opened the magnum of champagne someone had given him. 'Well, well, well . . . a doctor, a peer of the realm – and with secretarial skills. Wow.'

Georgie giggled. 'Come on,' she said as she pulled away from Jez's embrace. 'We've got to go.'

'Where?'

Georgie's look embraced both men. 'Home.'

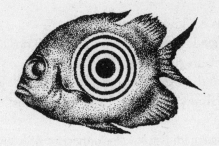

14

'What's this?' asked Dylan.

Georgie turned round. In the back seat of the Rolls, Dylan had the half-empty magnum in one hand and an envelope in the other. Oh damn, thought Georgie. Now I'm going to ruin a perfect day. 'Do you remember Mrs Ross?' she sighed.

'Mrs Ross? No.'

'InfoTec?' she prompted.

It was Jez who replied. 'Yes! The one who . . . er . . . well, our last customer.'

'Yes. Well she somehow managed to find my address.' Georgie took the envelope from Dylan. 'She came round the other day and . . . well, asked me to give this to you, Jez.'

'What is it?'

'I think it could be a writ.'

Jez grimaced. 'Just when we thought all our dreams had come true. Can you open it?'

Georgie did as she was bid. 'Oh my God!' she said as she read. 'Oh my God . . . I can't believe this!'

'Bad?'

Georgie giggled. 'Quite the opposite. She says that the circuit diagram you drew worked . . . she wants to license the VerbaTec chip.'

Jez nearly crashed the car. Dylan reached forward and hugged him. Another near crash.

'Look,' said Georgie, pointing at the wall they had narrowly missed. 'If you really must crash the car, I'd rather you didn't do it into our wall.'

'Our wall?' Jez and Dylan looked round. It was the same wall they had been following for what seemed like miles; it snaked along the side of the country road, an impervious barrier against the outside world.

Then Jez and Dylan looked at each other.

'For heaven's sake!' screamed Georgie as the car slewed across the road. 'Keep your eye on the road!' Then, a moment later, she instructed Jez to turn right.

'I thought you wanted me to keep my eye on the road.'

'Not any more. I want you to turn right.'

Jez flicked the indicator. He very nearly flicked it off again when he saw where he was heading. Then he looked at Georgie. 'You don't mean . . . ?'

A slow smile was playing at the corners of Georgie's mouth. 'I do.'

Dylan gasped. Ahead of them as they turned were twin stone lodges flanking vast wrought iron gates surmounted by a coat of arms. One of the gates was open, revealing a winding driveway and acre upon acre of rolling parkland.

'This,' stammered Dylan, 'is . . . your . . . family . . . home?'

'Well, it's a bit rundown.' Georgie was beginning to look flustered. 'You'll see in a minute.'

But it took longer than a minute. Jez and Dylan were reduced to an awed silence as they purred through the park, past a great lake on one side and a herd of deer on the other, then up a small incline and down again. More parkland greeted them, more undulating greenery punctuated by ancient oaks and elegant elms.

Then they rounded the final corner. Dylan nearly had a heart attack. Jez nearly crashed the car. In front of them, at the end of a sedately straight section of the drive, was one of the most beautiful stately homes they had ever seen. Magnificent and imposing, it possessed all the features they had ever dreamed of. There was a cupola; there was a vast pillared portico; there were symmetrical wings fanning out from the massive central block. At the end of one wing was a huge stable block, at the end of the other a glass orangery. And surrounding the whole were great sweeping lawns and colourful parterres.

Georgie coughed. 'See? It's a little unkempt.'

'Frightful mess.' Dylan was recovering his wits. 'Let's turn back and look for another one.'

Georgie giggled.

Jez was still unable to speak. All he could do was stare at the edifice in front of him. Then, as he swept into the enormous, circular expanse in front of the building, the front door opened and people began to pour out. They were laughing, yelling, cheering and clapping. And they were swarming towards them.

'Who on earth . . . ?' began Dylan.

'The children from the foundation.'

'But some of them are adults?'

Georgie shrugged. 'Staff.'

Staff. Of course. 'Hey! But that's the vicar who did Auntie Lesley's cremation!'

'Ah,' said Georgie. 'Perhaps I can explain about that later . . .'

As they pulled to a halt, the people from the house began to form a line beside the great stone balustrade of the portico.

'Oh God,' said Georgie, as she opened the door. 'This is getting embarrassing.'

Dylan and Jez looked not so much embarrassed as frightened. They looked in desperate need of reassurance.

'Come on,' said Georgie. 'They won't bite you.'

'I know.' Jez turned and looked straight into her eyes. 'Georgie?'

'Mmm?'

'I was wondering . . . well . . . would you . . . perhaps you might consider . . . or entertain . . .'

Dylan laughed and put an arm round each of their shoulders. 'He wants to know if you'll marry him.'

Georgie didn't reply at first. She simply stared, her face an inscrutable mask, at the man in front of her. 'I thought,' she said in a still, small voice, 'that –'

'Yes?'

Georgie flung herself into his arms. 'I thought you'd never ask!'

Dylan chuckled to himself. 'For heaven's sake – has the English aristocracy lost all sense of decency?'

Then, as he looked at the house again, he drew in a sharp, surprised breath. His heart missed a beat. Bells began to ring in his head; a host of angels came clamouring down from above. 'I certainly hope so,' he whispered to himself. 'I sure hope so.'

Floss had just emerged from the house. She stood still for a moment and then began to glide down the steps. Not for a second did her gaze falter. She was staring straight at Dylan. She continued to do so as she floated towards him, a radiant smile enhancing her startling beauty. Dylan was transfixed; totally enchanted by the vision of loveliness.

'Hello,' she said when she reached him.

'I do,' replied Dylan, already at the altar.

Epilogue

So the Impossible Dreams came true. Miss Van der Pump and Miss Biggins would have been extremely surprised. (The latter, in fact, would have been livid.) But those hapless ladies belong to the past, to the dusty compartment of Once Upon a Time.

Their erstwhile charges, on the other hand, lived Happily Ever After.

Cycle of Violence

Colin Bateman

'An Ulster Carl Hiaasen' *Mail on Sunday*

Bicycling journalist Miller is exiled from his big-city paper to small-town Crossmaheart. There, he is to replace another reporter, Jamie Milburn, who has disappeared – to no one's great surprise, since Crossmaheart is a notoriously fatal place in which to ask questions.

Miller aims to keep his head down, but as soon as he gets involved with Jamie's girlfriend Marie, that plan, and much else besides, begins to fall apart.

Darkly funny, romantic, disturbing and suspenseful, *Cycle of Violence* is the brilliant second novel from the author of the bestselling *Divorcing Jack*.

'Fast-paced, very black and very funny: Roddy Doyle meets Carl Hiaasen'   *Independent on Sunday*

'Terrific, mordant wit and a fine sense of the ridiculous . . . the writing is great'   *Evening Standard*

'Bateman's is the ultimate word on the insanity of the Troubles: no one has done it better'   *Scotland on Sunday*

ISBN 0 00 647935 9

The Dice Man

Luke Rhinehart

Let the dice decide!

This is the philosophy that changes the life of bored psychiatrist Luke Rhinehart – and in some ways changes the world as well.

Because once you hand your life over to the dice, anything can happen.

Entertaining, humorous, scary, shocking, subversive, *The Dice Man* is one of the cult bestsellers of our time.

'Touching, ingenious and beautifully comic'
ANTHONY BURGESS

'Brilliant . . . very impressive'   COLIN WILSON

'Hilarious and well written . . . sex always seems to be an option'   *Time Out*

ISBN 0 586 03765 9

Rogue Female

Nicholas Salaman

A book about living.
Dangerously.

He's shy, retiring and frightened. He's scared he'll be mugged, assaulted or spoken to by a female. Duncan Mackworth is scared of life. So he gets some help. He gets a personal instructor in self-defence. And more.

Duncan Mackworth doesn't know who to expect when he opens the door and he certainly isn't expecting a woman. A woman who will change Duncan Mackworth's life for ... well, for as long as it lasts.

'Salaman is a crisp, rather droll writer, capable of elegant flourishes at any moment'   *Sunday Telegraph*

ISBN 0 00 649029 8

Divorcing Jack

Colin Bateman

'Richly paranoid and very funny' *Sunday Times*

Dan Starkey is a young journalist in Belfast, who shares with his wife Patricia a prodigious appetite for drinking and partying. Then Dan meets Margaret, a beautiful student, and things begin to get out of hand.

Terrifyingly, Margaret is murdered and Patricia kidnapped. Dan has no idea why, but before long he too is a target, running as fast as he can in a race against time to solve the mystery and to save his marriage.

'A joy from start to finish . . . Witty, fast-paced and throbbing with menace, *Divorcing Jack* reads like *The Thirty-Nine Steps* rewritten for the '90s by Roddy Doyle' *Time Out*

'Grabs you by the throat . . . a magnificent debut. Unlike any thriller you have ever read before . . . like *The Day of the Jackal* out of the Marx Brothers' *Sunday Press*

'Fresh, funny . . . an Ulster Carl Hiaasen' *Mail on Sunday*

ISBN 0 00 647903 0

Melanie McGrath

Motel Nirvana

Dreaming of the New Age in the American Desert

'McGrath is a cool-eyed chronicler of a dispossessed generation – philosophical, astute and ultimately unforgiving. This
is no pseudo rock'n'roll trip, but an accessible and insightful
study of the modern condition. The final autobiographical
chapter is breathtaking.'   DEBORAH BOSLEY, *Literary Review*

'McGrath meets the nation's lost souls of the New Age. A 267-
year-old princess from the tribe of Atlantis, a technoshaman,
an alien who talks to Barbie dolls, an overweight angel
and a prince who will never die all impress her with their
certainties as much as they depress her with their chronic self-
awareness. It's an ambitious debut: McGrath has a keen sense
for deadpan descriptions of off-kilter encounters and an acute
knack for deflating the Myth.'   EMER BRIZZOLARA, *Ikon*

'McGrath has a fine, questing mind, a splendid eye for detail
and a healthy cynical attitude. Confronted at every turn – in
her deliciously sardonic picaresque travelogue through
America's south-western desert states – by the strange, the
sinister and the just plain barmy . . . she maintains a fine,
dense and colourful narrative that brings the desert landscape
and the loony-tune New Agers to life.'
NICK CURTIS, *Financial Times*

ISBN 0 00 654715 X

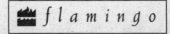